NO

Two friends about to discover
their libi...
they're r... ...on.

**Louise Jernigan (aka The Mom)**—... ...remember saying,
"How can the soul have rainbows if it never has tears?"
But after Wayne drives off, I'm euphoric and sad and
nostalgic and scared. All of a sudden I see myself
clearly—a past-middle-age widow who has lived her life
in the safe lane, suddenly thrust into the excitement and
roar of the fast lane, hanging on to her purse and hoping
she doesn't get sucked under and flattened.

**Patsy Leslie (aka Miss Sass)**—I know what people say
about me. Because of the way I carry on about men,
they think I'm a woman of vast experience. That's a
big fat lie. Women of my generation don't go in for
one-night stands: we're hoping for true romance and
lifetime commitment. A part of me has always believed
I'd find that kind of love again. In spite of my wayward
ways, it looks as if the universe is smiling on me.

# Peggy Webb

Although this Mississippi writer likes to think of herself as a pillar of her church, a civic leader and a shining star on the stage of Tupelo Community Theatre, her friends say she is as down-to-earth and zany as the characters she creates. When she talks about being former chairman of the Lee County Library Board of Trustees, a member of Tupelo Film Commission and other civic activities that would make a list longer than your leg, they point out that she was once seen in her front yard in nothing but socks and a T-shirt screaming about a snake in her rose garden. When she mentions how well she knows her way around roles such as M'Lynn in *Steel Magnolias*, Chick in *Crimes of the Heart* and the White Witch *in The Lion, the Witch and the Wardrobe*, they remind her that she once asked for directions to Wren and was told, "Lady, you're in Wren!"

Still, Peggy's friends love to sit on her front porch inhaling jasmine from her Angel Garden and celebrating her victories—bestseller lists, writing awards, options for film (*Where Dolphins Go*) and audiobooks (*Driving Me Crazy*).

When she's not writing, Peggy loves to play her vintage baby grand (especially blues), dig in her gardens and romp on her farm with her friend and faithful companion—her chocolate Labrador, Jefferson.

# PEGGY WEBB

# Confessions of a Not-so-Dead Libido

CONFESSIONS OF A NOT-SO-DEAD LIBIDO

Copyright © 2006 by Peggy Webb

i s b n - 1 3 : 9 7 8 - 0 - 3 7 3 - 8 8 1 1 6 - 1

i s b n - 1 0 :      0 - 3 7 3 - 8 8 1 1 6 - 9

TheNextNovel.com

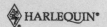

HARLEQUIN®

PRINTED IN U.S.A.

# From the Author

Dear Reader,

Once again I'm journeying into territory I love—the strong bonds of female friendship and the many ways we lift each other up when one of us forgets how to fly.

Sometimes a story starts in one direction and ends up going another. That's what happened with *Confessions of a Not-So-Dead Libido*. I thought I was writing about older women exploring their sexuality. Silly me! Patsy and Louise took over, as my characters always do, and showed me that this book is ever so much more than a woman ditching full-cut white cotton panties for black lace and push-up bras.

Make no mistake. Patsy and Louise romped and cavorted like sixteen-year-olds, but they also made me cry with the beauty and tenderness of their lifelong friendship.

Have fun reading, and do enter my contest. It's my way of saying, *Thank you for loving my books*. Details are on www.peggywebb.com.

Sincerely,

Peggy Webb

This book is for all my wonderful female friends who lift me up when I forget how to fly. You know who you are. Pour a glass of wine, sit on the front porch swing and know you are loved.

## ACKNOWLEDGMENTS

Many people deserve credit for this book:

My readers, whose letters inspire me

My family and friends, whose love sustains me

My wonderful agent, Evan Fogelman,
who is my cheerleader and biggest fan

My dream editor, Ann Leslie Tuttle,
who gave me the freedom to write with wings

My longtime friend Tara Gavin,
whose vision made the NEXT imprint possible

My magical unicorn,
who sprinkles stardust on my books…

Thank you. Without you, I am less.

## CHAPTER 1

*Louise*

**The** most exciting thing I've done in the past three years is give myself a pubic haircut. Last October in a frenzied attempt to perk myself up, I decided to lop off the straggly ends. Baring myself in front of a full-view mirror—Lord, that ought to be outlawed!—I snipped a little, just a half inch or so. I thought I'd end up looking cute and sassy down there. Instead I looked shorn. But the worst part was that it never grew back.

Well, no...the worst part was that I had to go to the gynecologist the following week. In a misguided moment (I have many of those) I tried to pass off my near-baldness as a joke.

"How do you like my sassy new cut?"

"I wouldn't notice if you dyed it green and tied it with a Christmas ribbon." Dr. Howard never even looked up.

I don't know what possessed me to say such a thing to him. For goodness sake! I'm the kind of woman who carries dental floss in her purse and raises her hand for permission to speak at Friends of the Library board meetings.

I guess I'm still a bit unhinged by grief. When I think about it, the most gut-wrenching aspect of my foolhardy foray with the shears is that *nobody is here to notice*.

I blame Roy. If my husband hadn't hauled off and died, he'd be here paying attention. He was that kind of man, the kind who doesn't go through life unaware but lives every moment with arms and heart and mind open wide.

My day didn't start until Roy pulled back the covers and said, "Wake up, Louise. Did you ever see such a morning?" Rain, shine, sleet or snow— the weather didn't matter. Roy pronounced each day "splendid."

My husband could see beauty in a mud puddle. Literally.

"Look at that, Louise," he'd say after a heavy spring rain. "Have you ever seen so many amazing colors in mud?"

I'd look and see nothing except brown. But he'd pick up a stick and swirl the mud till the colors of the earth emerged, terra-cotta and deep blue and coppery red, and all of a sudden I'd see the world through his eyes—extraordinary instead of mundane.

Roy was my mirror to life. Two years ago when he died, it cracked wide open, and I've been living a smashed-up, patched-together, sleepwalking life ever since.

If he were here on this balmy August night I'd be sailing with him on the Tenn/Tom Waterway to appreciate the full moon instead of baking cheese straws in preparation for Tuesday-night quilting club with Patsy. I'd be striving for sex appeal in Bermuda shorts and bare-toed sandals instead of opting for comfort in Reebok walking shoes and a twill skirt with enough elastic around the waist to make allowances for two helpings of lemon cream pie.

Not that I mind Patsy. Just the opposite. I love her. She's the only person besides Roy who creates wonder wherever she goes. (She creates mayhem, too, but we won't get into that.)

She's my mirror now, as well as my compass. Without Patsy sprinkling pixie dust and pointing the way, I'd fade into the wallpaper. And not the wild, jazzy kind either. I'd fade into a plain-Jane, gray-and-white-striped paper.

Of course, I have my daughter, Diana, but while I'm perfectly willing to let my friend be the captain of my leaky lifeboat, I refuse to be the kind of mother who defines herself through her children. Besides, she has her own life now, a husband and a baby on the way.

Independence is part of life's natural order. Eagles lay pointed sticks in the nest when it's time for the eaglets to leave home. And I suspect they have more sense than to hang around their children's new digs all the time just because they're lonely and suffering from empty-nest syndrome. Maybe a bit scared, too, but we won't go into that, either.

I arrange the last cheese straw on the cookie sheet, slide it into the oven then go into my office and open e-mail.

From: "Miss Sass" patsyleslie@hotmail.com
To: "The Lady" louisejernigan@yahoo.com
Sent: Tuesday, August 15, 6:00 p.m.
Subject: Dangerous Tonight
Hey Lady,
I'm feeling dangerous tonight. Hot to trot, if you know what I mean. Or can you even remember?? Look out, bridge club, here I come. I'm liable to end up dancing on the tables instead of bidding three spades. Whose turn is to drive, anyhow? Mine or thine?
XOXOX
Patsy
P.S. Lord, how did we end up in a club with no men?

This e-mail is typical Patsy. She's the only person I know who makes me laugh all the time. I guess that's why I e-mail her about ten times a day. She lives right next door. Wouldn't you think

I'd just pop over and sit down for a chat? Or pick up the phone and call several times a day?

I do both, but e-mail satisfies my urge to be instantly and constantly in touch with her without having to interrupt the flow of my life. If you call fifteen trips to the bathroom because I took a dieuretic to reduce the swelling in my feet "flow."

Sometimes we even save the good stuff, the real get-down-and-bare-your-soul talk, for e-mail. Don't ask me why. Maybe it's because e-mail gives you all the time you need to respond, plus it puts a buffer between you and the recipient if you need it.

From: The Lady, louisejernigan@yahoo.com
To: Miss Sass, patsyleslie@hotmail.com
Sent: Tuesday, August 15, 6:10 p.m.
Subject: Re: Dangerous Tonight
So, what else is new, Miss Sass? You're always dangerous. If you had a weapon, you'd be lethal.? It's your turn, and I hope you get the lead out of your foot because the last time you drove I nearly peed in my pants, which is more than a remote possibility tonight because I took a water pill and my bladder control's not what it used to be.

Hugs,

Louise

P.S. What's this about men? I thought you said your libido was dead?

I press Send then wait. Her reply is almost instantaneous.

"I knew you'd jump on that bait." Talking to myself is a habit I've acquired since Roy died.

From: "Miss Sass" patsyleslie@hotmail.com
To: "The Lady" louisejernigan@yahoo.com
Sent: Tuesday, August 15, 6:12 p.m.
Subject: Re: Dangerous Tonight
Ha! If I had a *brain* I'd be lethal.
And I said my libido was in hibernation, not DEAD!
Jeez, Louise!!!!!
P

Patsy loves to have the last word, so I shut off my computer.

She and I have been best friends for forty-five years. When she breezed into Tupelo, Mississippi, in a whirlwind of big hair and big attitude—a stunning blonde from Boise, Idaho, who looked like a fairy princess but talked like a truck driver— I was the only girl in fifth grade who would have anything to do with her. The rest were either scared or jealous, but I had nothing to be jealous about. I was a mousy-haired bookish nerd in glasses (still am, as a matter of fact).

How two such opposites became inseparable and remained that way for all these years is a mystery to me. I think the Universe saw my plight—a homely, motherless little girl with her head always in a book and a daddy who knew everything about computers but nothing about raising a daughter—and sent an angel to be my beacon. Not the prissed-up version that belongs in a church, but a sassy, down-to-earth one who knew nothing about wings and everything about flying.

I told Patsy this when we were twelve, and she said, "If you ever call me an angel again, I'm going to wash your mouth out with soap fifty times!"

I never did mention it again, but I've been flying along in her tailwinds ever since we met. When I feel myself plummeting, I call her.

She's the only person in the world I would phone in the middle of the night to say, "Did you ever get the feeling you grew up and turned into the wrong person?"

Last night I did that, and instead of asking me if I had lost my mind or pointing out that it was eleven and she'd been in bed since the ten-o'clock news, she said, "I know exactly what you mean. Ever since Rocky had the bad judgment to get electrocuted in a thunderstorm I've felt as if I was living somebody else's life."

Rocky was Patsy's first husband, the love of her life. I don't think she'll ever fly as high as she did when he was alive.

When we were ten I was going to be a poet and Patsy was going to be a movie star and we were going to live forever. By the time we were twelve our ambitions had elevated to President of the United States (me) and world-renowned figure skater (Patsy), never mind that the only ice Tupelo ever has is on the highways during a rare below-freezing drop in temperature right after a heavy rain. Patsy always was the fanciful one.

At seventeen we had shifted into reality mode. She aspired to be Mrs. Rocky Delgado and metaphorically fly to the moon while I aspired to be a teacher and travel the world.

Who would have dreamed the unexpected, meandering paths our lives would take? I think it all started when Patsy married Rocky. We were sitting on the steps of the band hall at Tupelo High when she told me her plans to elope. Though I used every weapon in my arsenal, including self-pity (I can't go to college without you. Who will be my roommate?) she married him anyway.

"All I want is Rocky and a singing career," she told me, and I could see why. Gorgeous and enormously talented, she had the potential to shoot straight to stardom. "We're going to New Orleans and Rocky is going to work on off-shore drilling rigs while I launch a career in the night-clubs. If Pete Fountain and Louis Armstrong could do it, so can I."

"I'm going to miss you."

"You'll do fine without me."

"You're the one who will do fine, not me."

She was right and I was wrong, but I didn't find that out until five years later. I was teaching English in Japan when Patsy's panicked call came.

"Oh, God, Louise. Rocky's gone."

"He left you? I can't believe that."

Over the years her calls had been ecstatic and her letters filled with exclamation points. "Rocky is the most glorious man alive!" "I'm singing at LuLu's! Well, serving drinks, too, but what does it matter!" "We've got the cutest apartment in the French Quarter!" "Sex with my Rocky is unbelievable!!!" And three months ago: "I'm pregnant!"

Although Patsy sounded as if she were right there in my rented room in Fukuoka, nothing seemed real except my landlord, Mr. Shimaoka, in his Zen garden below my window.

"He's dead, Louise. Struck by lightning in the parking lot of Piggly Wiggly. Oh God…what am I going to do?"

"Hang on, Patsy. I'll be right there."

"But you have your dream job."

"If you think I'm going to let my best friend

have a baby all by herself, you've sadly underestimated me, Patsy Delgado."

Now the smell of cheese straws lures me into the kitchen where I open the oven door and peek inside. A few more minutes, and they'll be done. I sit at the kitchen table to wait.

Who would have thought Patsy and I would both be widowed at fifty-five? And Patsy twice!

The only comfort I can find in my husband's death is that his heart gave out on the deck of our thirty-six-foot yacht, the *Louise*. If Roy had to die young, I'm glad he was on the boat. That man loved water so much I used to tease him that he was going to grow fins.

I'll never forget his excitement when we got our first boat, a sixteen-foot Bass Tracker with a Johnson outboard engine, a depth fish-finder and a trolling motor. A huge extravagance for newlyweds who didn't even own a house.

We saw it at a boat show in Memphis. "That's too much," Roy said when he saw the price tag.

"Let's get it."

"You mean that?"

"Yes. I never have believed in postponing good times till the price is right. If we wait till we think we can afford it, we'll be either too old to enjoy the boat or dead."

That was a lesson I learned over and over after Rocky's death.

"We can't afford to go out and buy shrimp Po-boys," I remember telling Patsy about two months after I'd moved to New Orleans. "The rent's due next week, and we barely have enough money to cover it."

I'd left Japan in the middle of the school term, so I was selling shoes for minimum wage while she was still parading around at LuLu's, covering her pregnancy by draping herself with sequined capes and ostrich plumes.

"The trouble with you, Louise, is that you don't trust the net."

"What net?"

"The net that always appears when you jump. It's called taking a leap of faith."

"Are you getting religion?"

"No, I'm just trying to get something to eat."

We got the Po-boys and Patsy proved her theory by making more than enough in tips that night to cover the cost.

When I asked how she did it, five months pregnant, she said, "It's a matter of perception. By the time I'd finished sweet-talking the good-ol' boys at LuLu's, they thought I had Fort Knox under these feathers and was fixing to give them the key."

The oven timer calls me back from my memories, and I take out the cheese straws then eat two while they're hot. They're so good I eat three more.

On the way to the bathroom I nab one last cheese straw, acutely aware of the heaviness of my step on the polished parquet floor and the ticking of the grandfather clock in the hallway—time moving on, sweeping me along in a path without Roy. Instead of dwelling on this I pop the cheese straw in my mouth and savor the warm, buttery, cheesy taste.

Calories disguised as comfort. What my life has become.

*Patsy*

**Naturally** I burned the brownies I'm taking to bridge club. If I were Louise I'd make a fresh batch. From scratch instead of using a mix. Heck, I'd never have burned them in the first place.

But I'm not Louise, or anybody who can even hold a candle to her. So I take a knife and scrape the burned part off and thank my lucky stars I had sense enough to cook food that's supposed to be black anyhow. The burned parts hardly even show.

I have better things to do than act like Suzi Homemaker. Paint my toenails, for one. Even if I don't have anybody to appreciate the fact that I chose passion purple.

"'You can take the girl out of the honky-tonk,

but you can't take the honky-tonk out of the girl,'"
I sing as I dump the burned treats onto a paper plate
and wrestle with the plastic wrap. Finally I give up
and use tin foil. But not before I say, "Kiss my foot."

Ordinarily I'd have said, "Kiss my butt," but
I'm trying to clean up my act because women
fixing to be a grandma for the first time need to
set a good example.

I hate to be outdone by something as small as
plastic wrap that won't unroll, but lately these
little aggravations throw me. Used to be it would
take a Brahmin bull to unravel Patsy Hawkins.
Well, make that Patsy Hawkins Delgado Leslie,
twice married and looking for number three.

What I ought to do is stay home tonight, sit
down at the piano and turn my impromptu song
into a real one, but of course I know I won't do any
such thing. I have no discipline, no backbone, no
fire in my belly.

I used to, back when I was sixteen and my world
was defined by music and Louise Laney and Rocky
Delgado. Lord, when he moved to Tupelo full of
song and big Chicago ideas and big laughter, the

three of us were going to set the world on fire. Louise did. She graduated at the top of our class, then won every honor there was to win down at Mississippi State University.

But Rocky and I got bushwhacked by life. If it hadn't been for Louise giving up her dream job in Japan and coming to New Orleans to take care of me, I'd probably have had Josh in a sugarcane field. And Lord only knows how I would have gotten through the grief without her.

I know this sounds like a three-handkerchief opera—a pregnant young widow and her best friend in a low-rent apartment trying to make ends meet—but it was more like *The Odd Couple*. There I was parading around with a belly as big as a watermelon, singing at LuLu's lounge and thriving on everything gaudy, bawdy and socially unacceptable, while she was correct and upright in every way, a cross between Miss Manners and Queen Victoria. I'd come home and flop on the sofa to gorge on chocolate-covered cherries, then hide the wrappers and the box from Louise.

I never could fool her about my hiding places.

She could sniff out chocolate better than a French pig rooting out truffles.

"You've got to quit that, Patsy, and start eating right." She'd march in the kitchen and pour me a glass of milk, then priss down the fire escape to dump my forbidden chocolates in the garbage can in the back alley.

"I'll quit it if you will," I told her.

"Quit what?"

"Acting like an old maid. Go out and have a good time."

"I'm having a good time."

"Yeah, slave labor at Jacobson's Department Store."

"Did I tell you about—"

"If you're trying to sidetrack me, you failed."

Of course, she hadn't. Louise could always distract me with her stories. She has a knack for instant connection with strangers and a wonderful sense of the ridiculous.

She's also a rock, a brick, my Statue of Liberty, my hero. I don't know what I'd do without her.

As I dump the brownies in a paper sack and

head to the bathroom to put on makeup, I marvel at how somebody as classy as Louise has remained my truest friend for forty-five years.

She's smart and educated and always knows exactly what to say in every situation, even the tough ones. Last summer when we got stranded at the airport in San Francisco on the way back from Hawaii and had to stand in a line about six miles long to get booked on another flight, I told a rude (to say the least) man behind me to "go take a flying leap into a pile of horse manure." Only I didn't say *manure*; I said *shit*. If Louise hadn't intervened I'd probably have ended up in a West Coast jail. (She has to pull my chestnuts out of the fire with depressing regularity.) What she did was make up a cock-and-bull story about me suffering severe depression on account of the recent death of my second husband.

I never suffer severe depression. While I felt a certain sadness over poor old Bill's demise, my biggest emotion was guilt because I never did love him the way I loved Rocky.

Louise may be the only person in the world who

understands this. I used to hope some of her intelligence and class would rub off on me, but it never did.

Bill tried to turn me into a Louise clone. You know, somebody proper who gets picked as president of the Garden Club and hosts fancy teas in a gazebo surrounded by roses so his real estate clients would be impressed. I flunked Garden Club 101 and played the wrong kind of music, country and western, at my one and only attempt at gracious entertaining, so Bill finally said, "Forget it. Just don't wear short shorts and spike heels in the grocery store, is all I ask."

I cleaned up my dress but I never could clean up my act. I was born bad and on the wrong side of the tracks while Louise was born with a silver spoon in her mouth and a gold good-conduct medal pinned to her butt.

In addition she never loses her temper, which I do in spite of my good intentions—and with such force the neighborhood's small dogs cower under their porches for days afterward.

I've even been accused of giving Mrs. Carlson's pampered poodle a heart attack. And while I

wouldn't call that an outright lie, I would say it's
stretching the truth.

When Mrs. Carlson moved, I told Louise it was
because of me. But she said, "You give yourself too
much credit. She moved so she wouldn't have to
drive all the way to Memphis to see her psychiatrist."

"I'll take credit for that, too. I've been known
to drive people crazy."

"Who?"

"Bill, for one."

"You did not."

"Yes, I did. He used to say so all the time."

"Jackass."

That's the only time I've ever heard Louise use
an unladylike word. She's a friend worth dying for.

Thank God, I don't have to die for her, just pick
her up in five minutes because if I don't, we'll be
late or I'll have to speed, and either way, Louise
won't like it. Oh, she won't say so. She's too much
a lady to complain. But I can always tell. She'll
stiffen up like a mannequin and sit tight-lipped on
her side of the car like she's waiting for execution.

See, this is what I love about close friendship—knowing each other's quirks and secrets. I'm probably the only person in the world, including her daughter, who knows that Louise would as soon throw herself in front of a train than go to bed without her mascara. Most women take great pains to remove the gunk, but not Louise.

It's her one small vanity. Lord, she barely even uses lipstick. I've told her she'd look ten years younger if she'd slash some red on her lips, but she won't listen to me. She's stubborn as a butt-headed mule.

As if to prove my point, here she comes without a smidgen of lipstick, wagging a handwoven picnic hamper and wearing a skirt that looks as if it came over on the Mayflower and a pair of Reebok walking shoes that I know good and well are five years old. I was with her when she bought them.

She settles into the passenger side of the car. This takes a while because of the bulky hamper.

"Good God, Louise. You look like you're going to a Baptist tent revival."

"Just hush and drive."

She gives my graying French twist, my slacks and red cotton sweater set the once-over, and never says a word, just arches her eyebrow in an all-knowing way.

"I saw that," I tell her.

"What?"

"You know perfectly well what. That supercilious eyebrow."

If I were in her shoes I'd have some smart-aleck remark, but Louise just grins.

"Well, all right," I say. "I'll admit it. I've toned down."

"Toned down? You've made a complete metamorphosis."

Louise means this as a compliment, but I get this twitchy feeling like somebody who is not in her own skin.

I did this deliberately, let Bill change me into a Stepford Wife version of myself. It was the least I could do for a man who married a woman with a three-year-old and a doubtful future and became a wonderful father to my son. But still, I miss the old, flamboyant me.

Now I say to Louise, "It's about time, don't you think? Since I'm fixing to be a grandma."

"Can you believe it?" Louise says. "We're having a grandbaby."

"I'm flabbergasted."

And that's the God's truth. How I ever got lucky enough to have a brilliant, sensible, successful son like Josh is beyond me. If he didn't have Rocky's dark good looks I'd swear he was switched at birth and left with me by mistake.

That he ended up marrying Louise's darling Diana is one of those amazing gifts of the Universe that makes me believe in grace.

If I were a good person I'd show my gratitude by performing daily acts of charity. But I'm a shallow woman whose only act of charity is to use mouthwash after I eat garlic so my bridge partner won't faint.

I wheel my red Jaguar through Highland Circle, hoping everybody's looking. When Mary Jo Barton's house comes into view, Louise says, "Don't raise my bid unless you have the cards to back it up."

"When have I ever?"

"Every time we play."

"Maybe I'll quit playing with you. Let you find a new partner. How'd you like them apples?"

"Oh, hush up and park the car. You know I don't want another partner."

"Well, okay then. You tend to your bids and I'll tend to mine."

Louise lets me have the last word—as always—then we walk arm in arm up the sidewalk for a scintillating evening of counting tricks and over-indulgence in fattening foods.

*Louise*

I scrub my face, leaving on my mascara in spite of the fact that Roy's not here, then put on one of his old shirts and my favorite baggy pajama bottoms and try not to notice that the once-white shirt is now turning yellow.

What I need is instant connection. What I need to say is, Hey, I'm still here, I'm still me even if there's no one in the house to see me breathe or hear me pray or feel the soft flesh of my inner thigh.

Reaching through cyberspace, I connect with the friend who always picks me up when I forget how to fly.

From: "The Lady" louisejernigan@yahool.com
To: "Miss Sass" patsyleslie@hotmail.com
Sent: Tuesday, August 15, 9:45 p.m.
Subject: Bridge Club
Didn't you know we couldn't make three hearts with that lousy hand of yours? When are you going to start taking bridge seriously?
Louise, who really wanted to win

I know better than to walk off and leave the computer because Patsy and I usually end our evenings this way. Sometimes I wonder how I would keep going if weren't for her sassy e-notes.

From: "Miss Sass" patsyleslie@hotmail.com
To: "The Lady" louisejernigan@yahoo.com
Sent: Tuesday, August 15, 9:50 p.m.
Subject: Kiss my foot!
See above.
Patsy, who doesn't give a fart in a whirlwind about winning a bridge game but who really, really

would like to finish the cheese straws you gave me in peace!

I turn off the computer, climb into bed, pull the sheet under my chin and wonder if Patsy and I are settling gracefully into old age or merely settling.

## CHAPTER 3

*Patsy*

**My** alarm clock goes off at the godawful hour of six a.m., and now I'm the one reaching for Reeboks. I envy Louise being able to sleep late, while I trudge off to my job at Merchants and Farmers Bank.

But *no*, do you think she's sleeping? When I go into the kitchen for my lazy woman's breakfast— a honey bun zapped in the microwave and instant Folgers—her kitchen light is already on. I glance out the window so I can wave if she's looking. She's not, so I take down a coffee mug I got on vacation with Bill in Portsmouth, New Hampshire, that says "Live Free or Die."

Good advice if you can take. I used to, but after Rocky died I quit, so I guess I'm as good as dead.

Thirty-four years ago if you'd told me I'd end up being a bank teller with a social life that included nothing more than bridge on Tuesday and quilting on Thursday, I'd have crawled in a cave and pulled a stone over the door.

God has a sense of humor, that's all I can say.

With the mug in one hand and a honey bun in the other, I turn on the computer and e-mail Louise.

From: "Miss Sass" patsyleslie@hotmail.com
To: "The Lady" louisejernigan@yahoo.com
Sent: Wednesday, August 16, 6:20 a.m.
Subject: Waxing philosophical
Tell me again why I decided to wait thirty years before retiring from my job at the bank. Tell me why I took a shitty job I hate in the first place. Sometimes I think we've both settled into a rut as comfortable as our full-cut cotton panties.
Hugs,
Patsy, with an itch that needs scratching

I'm getting ready to turn off the computer when Louise's reply pops up.

From: "The Lady" louisejernigan@yahoo.com
To: "Miss Sass" patsyleslie@hotmail.com
Sent: Wednesday, August 16, 6:23 a.m.
Subject: Re: Waxing philosophical
Because you've got only one more year to go,
that's why. Just think how much bigger your retire-
ment check is going to be! Besides, you have a
good job.
And don't get me started. Last night when I
crawled into bed with Roy's empty pillow I felt as
worn-out and useless as my old blue terry cloth
house shoe your cat stole and chewed to pieces.
Maybe we are in a rut, but it's the only place I know
to be right now.
And for Pete's sake, forget about that itch. Every
time you get an itch, you get in trouble. Get out
"Old Faithful."
XOXO
Louise, who wouldn't know how to scratch if I itched.

Good Lord, she's driving me crazy. You'd think
she'd been buried along with Roy. Two years is too
long to mope and carry on, and I've told her so.

Let's face it, she's smarter and classier, but I
adjusted to widowhood faster.

From: "Miss Sass" patsyleslie@hotmail.com
To: "The Lady" louisejernigan@yahoo.com
Sent: Wednesday, August 16, 7:27 a.m.
Will you forget about that old shoe? You had no business leaving it on the back porch.
And for your information, I wore out "Old Faithful" six months ago. Let's take a road trip down to Fantasy Land in Columbus this Saturday. I might replace "Old Faithful" with one that's hot pink and glows in the dark.
XOXO
P, off to the salt mines

After I dress, I dash to my Jag, then back out of the driveway. This daily grind is my own fault. If I hadn't squandered Bill's money on diamonds and flashy cars, I'd be in Mexico City drinking margaritas and doing the flamenco instead of roaring through Tupelo trying to get to work on time without getting a speeding ticket.

The thought of trying to sweet-talk a traffic cop at my age makes me sweat. Of course, I'd be sweating anyhow because August in Mississippi is hotter than blazes. By the tag end of summer my yard looks a testing ground for government missiles. (I do, too, but we won't go into that.)

Louise is getting her paper, and I wave when I pass by. Standing on her white-columned front porch between two pots of perfect pink geraniums she looks like an advertisement for gracious Southern living, which just goes to show you can't judge other people by how they look. Sure, Louise is a genuine lady, a two-page color layout in an uppity-up magazine, but Josh and I are proof that she's got guts and steel under that prettied-up, sanitized demeanor.

I'll never forget the day he was born. Lord, it was raining so hard in New Orleans you couldn't see your hand in front of your face. Louise was still in the shoe department, working the evening shift, and I was so big I'd stopped working altogether.

There I was, sitting in that little three-room apartment planning to enjoy an evening away from the chocolate Nazi (Louise), when the first labor pains hit. Thanks to Lamaze classes (and to Louise who had dragged me there), I wasn't worried. Instead I relaxed on the couch and dug into the chocolate cherries.

Labor contractions hit two hours before she was due home and escalated so rapidly I didn't think about the phone, the doctor, the storm outside. All I did was pray Louise would hurry. By the time she got home I was writhing and carrying on like a dying calf in a hailstorm.

"Good God, Patsy..." Louise steamrolled through a path of chocolate wrappers without uttering a single recriminatory word. "We've got to get you to a hospital."

About that time the Nile River gushed all over the couch.

"This baby's not fixing to wait. You've got to deliver it, Louise."

For the first time in her life, she was struck speechless and helpless. If I didn't snap her out of it I was fixing to have to get this whale through a keyhole all by myself.

"'Lawdy, Miss Scarlett,'" I said. "'I don't know nothin' about birthin' babies.'"

"Have you lost your mind?" Louise leaped to the couch and put her hand on my forehead.

"My head's not where it hurts."

"Well, quit acting like Prissy and start doing your breathing exercises. I have stuff to do."

Louise whirled into action, and I knew everything was going to be all right.

I don't know that now. If passion were motor oil she'd be about a quart low. And lately I'm having a hard time finding the fuel tank, so who am I to talk?

Still, call me sexist all you want, but I know what I know: Louise needs a man. Of course, every time she's around the opposite sex she has her prickly spurs on.

On the other hand, I roll out the welcome mat (not that anybody since Bill has crossed the threshold). I'm not dead yet, even if some folks (otherwise known as neighborhood busybodies) think I ought to act as if I am.

Just last week Irma June Lipincott, who lives on the other side of me and is always spying, saw me in my swimsuit and said it wasn't "seemly" for somebody whose husband had been dead only a year to parade herself around like that.

She stomped off, miffed. I guess she'd have had

a heart attack if she knew I was fixing to take off the top so I wouldn't have tan lines.

You never know. Somebody interesting might come into my life and notice.

Well, wouldn't you know? The only person who notices me today is my immediate supervisor, Janet Hoover, also known as Herbert, but not by anybody except me. She's standing by the watercooler tapping her foot and looking at her watch.

"You're two minutes late, Patsy."

"So sue me" is what I want to say, but since I'm fond of eating and the phone company would disconnect me if I didn't pay the bills, I say, "Traffic," which is a big fat lie.

There's very little traffic between my little neighborhood and the corner of Main and Green. But Herbert must have other things on her mind (probably sniffing out another criminal type who's taking an illegal coffee break) because she trundles off without so much as raising her eyebrow.

Everybody with any sense is home under the air conditioner with a tall glass of lemonade, so this turns into one of those mornings that whiz by with the speed of a broken-footed turtle. I start counting the minutes till my coffee break and am just fixing to turn my window over to Susie Jones when a cross between Gregory Peck and John Wayne walks through the door.

With his combed-back wavy black hair he looks like a Mississippi riverboat gambler, and the way he swaggers as he heads my way, he ought to be wearing a ten-gallon hat and a pair of six-shooters.

I am instantly intrigued. He reminds me of Rocky, the kind of man who electrifies a room. A little part of me that has been anesthetized for a very long time springs to life. I want to jump up and shout, See, See! There is life after fifty!

Oh, I know what people say about me. Because of the way I carry on about men, they think I'm a woman of vast experience. The mean-spirited ones even say I've been around the block more than once. That's a big fat lie.

I've had only two men in my life—Rocky and Bill. Women of my generation don't go in for one-night stands; we're hoping for true romance and lifetime commitment.

I might have mistaken my respect and deep regard for Bill as true love if there had never been a Rocky. But there was. And I know the kind of soul connection we had is rare—probably once in a lifetime. Still, a part of me has always believed I'd find that kind of love again.

In spite of my wayward ways, it looks as if the universe is smiling on me. *Lord, if you'll let him come my way I'll ring the bell for the Salvation Army's Christmas kettle.*

I feel safe making this promise. December is a long way off, which gives me plenty of time to reform.

"Patsy..." Susie taps me on the shoulder. "Are you ready for your coffee break?"

I'd sprout dangling nose hair before I'd turn this man over to a woman who looks like Marilyn Monroe, only red-haired, which makes her bombshell looks even more appealing.

"You'd better handle that customer heading toward the vault first."

She hurries off, thank God, and I pinch my

cheeks to add a little color. When the intriguing stranger gets close enough I drag out my sexiest, lounge singer's voice.

"May I help you?"

It gets them every time. He strides up to my window and props his elbow there as if he's fixing to buy the bank.

"As matter of fact, you can. I've just moved here…"

There's a god of second chances, after all. Or third, but who's counting.

"I want to set up an account."

"I will personally see that you get VIP service."

Rounding the bank of tellers' windows, I tell Laura Lee Holcomb to cover for me, that I'm on break.

Then I lead the way toward New Accounts, swaying my hips and wafting perfume for all I'm worth. I knew someday my training at LuLu's would come in handy. The hips and the perfume made customers drop big tips every time.

Who knows what will drop by the time I finish with Mr. Potential Hero.

*Louise*

I can't believe school will be back in session next week. Even more, I can't believe I'm still teaching English in Room 21 at Tupelo High.

The room is empty now and I'm standing here smelling chalk dust and holding a greasy bag of cream-filled doughnuts. Where did all the years go? What happened to the starry-eyed idealist who was going to travel the world teaching then come home, get a Ph.D., become a school principal and publish scholarly articles with lofty titles such as "The Transgender Paradigm Shift Toward Free Expression" and "Asian-American Panethnicity: Bridging Identities and Institutions"?

My cell phone rings and I dig around in my purse till I find it. It's Aunt Charlotte, Daddy's sister and my only living link to him—except one male cousin who lives in Idaho and hardly ever comes home unless he wants money.

"Louise, Bradley's trying to take my tractor keys. You've got to tell that old fart I'm not too old to drive the John Deere. If he thinks he's getting these keys, he's got another think coming."

"Slow down, Aunt Charlotte. Did Uncle Bradley give a reason?"

Daddy died after a long, heartbreaking slide into the oblivion of Alzheimer's, and I'm always checking to make sure Aunt Charlotte is not in its dark grasp.

"I got stuck and it upset him."

"Where did you get stuck?" She doesn't answer, and I say, "Aunt Charlotte? What are you not telling me?"

"Well, all right. I got stuck in the lake. But I was only halfway in."

Dear Lord. "I'll come over after lunch and we'll talk about it."

"Won't do you a lick of good, but come on anyway. I've got a bone to pick with you."

I know what that bone is, and I don't look forward to picking it. Ever since Roy died, Aunt Charlotte has wanted me to sell my house and move in with her and Uncle Bradley.

*Sure*, I get lonesome and I love the farm and

they're getting old and will soon need somebody. Still, giving up my life—even if it is a bit on the skimpy side—would feel like giving up entirely. I might as well just knit myself an afghan, sit down in a rocking chair and wait for Gabriel to toot his horn.

Taking a dust cloth out of my briefcase, I start wiping my desk. (My scintillating life as I know it.) Although Tupelo High has a perfectly capable custodial staff, every August I come here to tidy up my room and get it ready for the next group of juniors and seniors. They'll sit in precise rows in front of me, each filled with his own expectations, and I'll stand right where I am now, exactly where I've stood for the past twenty-eight years.

Dust cloth abandoned, I sit at my desk in my swivel chair and open a Dunkin' Donut bag and pull out a cream-filled confection. The first sugary bite slides down my throat like a sigh, and the second fills an empty place in me that lately has been growing at such alarming speed I fear I'm going to vanish.

I lick the sugar off my fingers, planning to stop at one. Really, I'm stopping.

I even close the bag. The sun shining through

the high-ceilinged windows sets dust motes dancing around the empty chairs—a metaphor for my life. I reach into the bag for a second. Then a third. A fourth.

I had planned to be good, really I had, but lulled by the smell of sugar and chalk dust and lemon oil wafting up from the old wooden floor, I eat until I finish the whole bag.

Wishing won't change a thing. I am past my prime and Roy is gone and nothing has turned out the way I thought it would. Except Diana and Patsy, and for that I am unutterably grateful.

"Mom?"

The sound of my daughter's voice startles me. Madonna-like, Diana stands in a path of sunlight that turns her blond hair into a halo. She's Roy made over, beautiful from head to toe, the baby-made bulge in her belly enhancing her shining appeal.

"Are you ready for lunch?"

"Well…" I crumple the bag and shove it into the desk drawer, but not before she sees it. I can tell by the look of concern that crosses her face. "Sure, I guess I could eat a salad or something."

Instead of chastising me about my lack of self-control and my terrible eating habits, Diana pats my arm and says, "Is Finney's Sandwich Shop all right with you? I need to get back to the clinic in an hour."

She and Josh own a physical therapy clinic on the corner of Highway 6 and Eason Boulevard, and they're both the kind of people who would never keep a patient waiting. All I can say is that Patsy and I outdid ourselves with our children, and that's not bragging. Diana and Josh make me want to stand on a hill and shout, "See, everything's going to be all right, the future's in good hands."

We head to Finney's Sandwich Shop in Diana's black Jeep because she doesn't like the way I drive. Neither does Patsy.

I'm no longer paying attention. My mind wanders off. Sometimes it goes to the Camden, Maine, where Roy and I spent our last vacation, most of it on Penobscot Bay in a rented sailboat. But mostly it goes to the last time we made love. It was early Saturday morning before he left for what turned out to be his last day on the water. The sun was pouring through the skylight when we woke up, and we turned to each other at the same time, hungry to share the absolute beauty of morning. We ended up crosswise on the bed with the sheet tangled around our legs and our hearts pounding against each other.

It was a kind of connection that transcends the physical and feels like worship. Only three other times have I felt that way—when I delivered Josh, when I gave birth to Diana and when Casey Posey wept at the lyric beauty of Pat Conroy's prose.

Casey is six-three, a former running back for Tupelo High, and as he sat in my classroom in his wheelchair, his crushed legs dangling and his eyes filled with tears, I whispered, "Thank you." Just that. Thank you for a God revealed in an embrace, a baby's cry and a single teardrop.

Now my daughter is saying to me, "Mom, Josh and I will be in Memphis this weekend at a physical therapists' conference, so we won't be there for Sunday dinner."

Sunday dinner has been a tradition for the Jernigans and the Leslies since Patsy and I married Bill and Roy, at first, alternating between Patsy's house and mine and now adding the third rotation at Diana's. I love it that we keep this tradition alive. We're weaving the years into a tapestry that will be treasured for generations to come. At least, I hope so.

"That's okay. Patsy and I will carry on."

"You always do."

Just the mention of Patsy's name makes you smile. I know this. Still, the flash of delight on Diana's face makes me wonder what people do when they hear my name. Wince? Say "Poor Louise"?

Lord, how did I turn into that kind of woman?

"So what are you going to name the baby?"

I mention this subject casually, as if Patsy and I haven't brought it up nearly every day since we learned we were going to be grandmas.

"We're not telling, and you and Aunt Patsy might as well hush about it."

We're lobbying for Patsy Louise if it's a girl. Patsy says the kids will cave in if we nag them enough, but I'm not one to nag. Just suggest.

"Well, you know my opinion on the matter, so I'm not saying another word."

"Good."

"Of course, having a grandchild named for its two grandmothers would be very nice."

Diana gives me this *look*, and I don't say anything else about the baby until I've got her cornered in the car.

"It's nice to honor the living," I say.

"Are you, Mom?"

"Am I what?"

"Living? I worry about you since Daddy died."

"Well, put your mind at ease. Patsy and I are doing great. Really."

By lumping Patsy in with me, I can say this without crossing my fingers behind my back. Patsy would do great if you dumped her in a briar patch with wild hogs.

I prefer not to think about my own state of mind. Instead I spend a couple of hours at the school's copying machine, then drive out to Birmingham Ridge on the north side of town for a bracing talk with Aunt Charlotte.

She greets me at the door in elastic waist denim pants, one of Uncle Bradley's old chambray work shirts and new combat boots, which she says are great for walking around the farm. (Patsy always hoots when Aunt Charlotte refers to their thousand-acre spread as "the farm.")

"How are you Aunt Charlotte?"

"I was out delivering a calf because Bradley can't pour piss out of a boot with the directions written on the heel."

"Why, Aunt Charlotte! That's not true. He was a brilliant doctor before he retired."

"Piffle. He's got all that book sense and not a lick of horse sense." She peers behind me like a little sparrow searching for a juicy worm.

"Where's Patsy?"

"She's still at work. Remember?"

"Don't look at me like I'm getting senile. Of course I remember. I just thought she might take off to visit me, that's all."

*Please God*, I say silently. Just that. *Please*.

"Come on in." Aunt Charlotte holds the door open. "I've got cookies if you can stand them. I can't cook worth a dime."

"Now, Aunt Charlotte."

"Don't you 'Now, Aunt Charlotte' me. Sit down and take a load off your feet. Tell me how come you don't stop rattling around in that big old empty house and move in with us. Patsy did."

Oh, Lord, here we go again. I sidestep.

"That was a long time ago, when Josh was a baby. Where's Uncle Bradley?"

"Visiting that old kook."

This is the only thing she ever calls Uncle Bradley's sister Bertha, even to her face.

"Be nice. She gave you a lovely present for your seventy-fifth birthday."

"Piffle. It came from the dollar store. I know quality."

Aunt Charlotte serves dark, rich coffee (Uncle Bradley keeps a pot going) and really awful cookies, and I remind myself to bring her a batch of oatmeal raisin cookies the next time I come.

Seeking to turn the subject away from my moving and Uncle Bradley's failures, I ask about my cousin.

"How's Jerry?"

"He's still on *Brokeback Mountain*."

Ever since the movie, that has been Aunt Charlotte's term for anybody who is not doing what she thinks he ought to be doing. In Jerry's case, this means he owns a package liquor store, he smokes, he's had four wives and he has no children.

"Aunt Charlotte, I've been thinking that Uncle Bradley's right about the tractor. You don't need to be on it. That's what Lefty's for."

Lefty Loredo has been her farm manager for years.

"You might as well save your breath. Lefty's retiring. Besides, I hid the keys. You need not think you can find them, either."

"I was just looking for my purse. I've got to go."

"Stay for supper. I haven't had a decent meal in two weeks. You can cook."

Why not? Nobody's waiting at home. I tie on a clean apron and start making pot roast, feeling needed and cocooned. This is the house and farm my granddaddy Lucas owned, the childhood wonderland I roamed with a dog named Tomorrow because I read that Audrey Hepburn had a cat by the same name. I loved that she would pick the cat up and say, "Tomorrow everything's going to be wonderful."

Daddy and I lived here after Mother died, but he never had any abiding interest in farming. His mind was always on the then-emerging technology of computers, so when Granddaddy Lucas died he left the farm to Aunt Charlotte, who loved it fiercely.

With my feet planted on the worn, lemon-oil-scented oak floors and my hands holding the same potato peeler my grandmother used, I feel connected to generations of Lucas family all the way back to Hiram, who set sail from Great Britain in 1635 and worked his way south from Boston.

This house echoes with who I am—my grandmother who equated love with food and served her soul and spirit to her family in a chocolate cherry cake; my grandfather who tethered himself to the Universe by burying his hands in the earth and nurturing apple trees and gardenia bushes and daffodils that sang of spring even while winter winds still chilled our bones; my father who cherished tradition and knowledge, and even my Aunt Charlotte who steams full speed into a task, no matter how messy or difficult or unconventional.

I'm lucky. I know that. And I'm going to start counting my blessings tomorrow. Really, I am.

## CHAPTER 4

*Louise*

**My** feet are tired when I get home from Aunt Charlotte's so I kick off my shoes before I check my e-mail.

From: "Miss Sass" patsyleslie@hotmail.com
To: "The Lady" louisejernigan@yahoo.com
Sent: Wednesday, August 16, 5:30 p.m.
Subject: WOW!!!!!
Where are you? Out having a high-heel time, I hope. Boy, do I have news for you. I met a hunk! I'm talking lip-smacking, drop-your-drawers gorgeous! And he's asked me out!!!!!
Hurry up and get home. I need to talk.
XOXOX
Patsy, With her motor revved and her pump primed

I can't believe this. Well, I can, really. Patsy's a beautiful woman, plus she's not the kind to be living such a quiet life.

But I just didn't think it would be this soon.

I'm not ready for this, and I'm not sure she is. Lord, I hope he's nice. What if he's the predatory kind you read about in the grocery store tabloids?

What am I going to say to her? Congratulations? That would be a huge fabrication. Until I know who this man is how can I congratulate her? And if I caution her, she might take it the wrong way.

This is awful. I've never worried about Patsy taking anything the wrong way.

Shaking off my misgivings I start typing.

From: "The Lady" louisejernigan@yahoo.com
To: "Miss Sass" patsyleslie@hotmail.com
Sent: Wednesday, August 16, 6:30 p.m.
Subject: Re: WOW!!!!!
What can I say? I'm floored. I want to know everything, and I mean EVERYTHING!
Louise

The doorbell starts ringing, so I punch *send* then hurry to the front door. There stands Patsy looking like something straight out of Las Vegas in too much mascara, a Lycra skirt up to her you-know-what and red sling-back shoes with heels so high I'm afraid she'll fall and break her neck.

"Thank God. I thought you'd never get home." She bustles in, her arms full of packages. "Just wait till you see what I bought."

I lead her to the den and flop down on the sofa. Limp, if you want to know the truth.

"Who is this man?"

"I'll get to that in a minute. I can't wait for you to see this." She rustles through a sack as big as Texas—from Victoria's Secret, no less!—and pulls out this little bitty pair of black lace bikinis that I couldn't fit over my big toe.

"What do you think?" She holds them in front of her brand-new miniskirt (obviously, since I've never seen it). "Is this perfect or what?"

"You mean *for what*. What are you planning to do? Seduce this man on your first date?"

"Well, I swear. If I didn't know better I'd say you're jealous."

"You know better."

"Yes, I do, so who stuck a cob up your butt?"

I never could fool Patsy about my moods, so I shift the blame to my profession.

"I was at the high school today getting ready for the fall semester."

"Hells bells, that explains it. I'd slit my throat if I had to face 120 hormone-pumped teenagers a day."

Patsy plops onto my La-Z-Boy recliner and raises the footrest. I can see up her skirt practically all the way to her peach blossom—which is what Aunt Charlotte called it when she told me about the birds and the bees. But that's what you'd expect from a woman who lives and breathes the fields and orchards of her farm.

If it hadn't been for Patsy I'd have gone to my wedding bed with a vague notion of bees pollinating a peach blossom. And now I'm fixing to lose her. If this new man is half the hunk she says, he's not going to be planning buffets for three at Western Sizzlin'.

"I also had dinner with Aunt Charlotte."

"What's that sassy little Julius Caesar up to?" Patsy jerks at the hem of her silly skirt which is bunching up around her middle.

"Birthing a calf," I say, and Patsy hoots. "Tell me about this man."

"He's new in town and I saw him first."

"Does he have a name?"

"He most certainly does, Miss Priss, and I ought to make you dig it out of me. You've had a sourpuss look on your face ever since I mentioned him."

"Well?"

"His name is Harry Thompson and he's a consultant on Tupelo's Fairpark development."

"How do you know? Maybe he's a con man. He just breezes into town and all of a sudden you're shopping at Victoria's Secret?"

"I swear, Louise, you ought to work for the Gestapo."

"I just don't want to see you get hurt. That's all."

"Jeez! I'm just going out to dinner with him. Not fixing to elope and set up housekeeping in Timbuktu."

"If you wear that outfit, there's no telling where you'll end up."

"Good God!" Patsy grabs the lever on my La-Z-Boy and sits bolt upright. "I'm not fixing to turn into a dried-up old fart."

"Stop it. You're going to make me pee in my pants." When I get on my high horse, Patsy always sidetracks me with laughter.

Now she's prancing around the room swinging her hips and posing.

"Will Harry like my rear action? What do you think, Louise?"

"I think you need a guitar and a black wig, and you can go on the road as an Elvis impersonator."

Plopping down beside me, she grabs two creamy butterscotch candies from the dish on the coffee table and hands one to me.

"I don't want you to worry. I was fixing to strut my stuff even before Harry came along. He just speeded up the process."

"I know, I know. I didn't mean to make you mad."

"I'm not mad, just horny. Don't you ever think about finding a man before you forget your math?"

"What does math have to do with it?"

"I mean, while you can still tell the difference between four inches and eight."

"Goofy." I punch her arm.

"Worrywart." She swats me back.

We started this exchange when we were ten. There's something wonderfully comforting about a familiar routine with your best friend.

"Listen," she says. "If it'll make you feel better, I won't wear the black lace panties on the first date."

"All right. I promise not to worry if you promise to wear full-cut white cotton."

"I not fixing to go Old Mother Hubbard. Let's compromise. How about pink silk with French-cut sides?"

"Done."

We both reach into the candy dish at the same time, then sit side by side eating sweets until Patsy starts yawning.

"I've got to get my beauty rest."

I wave goodbye at the door and watch until she's through the hedge and I see her porch light switch off, which indicates she's safely inside, then

I flip through the channels looking for a decent movie.

Wouldn't you know *Fatal Attraction* is on? The story of lovers who get done in by ice picks. I watch it anyhow. At least it's the woman who wields the ice pick. And if I know Patsy, in a situation such as this she'd be the one with the weapon.

After I turn off the TV, I check e-mail, knowing a note will be waiting.

From: "Miss Sass" patsyleslie@hotmail.com
To: "The Lady" louisejernigan@yahoo.com
Sent: Wednesday, August 16, 10 p.m.
Subject: Quilting Club
I forgot to tell you…tomorrow night's my big date, so I won't be going to quilting club. ? Eat enough for me, and if you take cheese straws save me some. Those were yummy!
Patsy, dreaming with my eyes wide open

I'm not fixing to hold back. Our friendship can survive the truth.

From: "The Lady" louisejernigan@yahoo.com
To: "Miss Sass" patsyleslie@hotmail.com
Sent: Wednesday, August 16, 10:30 p.m.
Subject: Re: Quilting Club
Just keep your feet on the ground and your legs together. That's all I ask.
Louise, who really, really wants you to be happy and SAFE
P.S. Cheese straw recipe attached.

After I go to bed I toss and turn, worrying over Patsy. Finally I get up and fix myself a bowl of Cheerios with real cream and two tablespoons of sugar. Cream and sugar are good for the soul. More people ought to know this. The world would be a better place.

I finish the bowl and think about fixing another, but I'm going to be strong. Really, I am.

If you want to know the truth, it's not the state of Patsy and the world I'm worrying about, it's me. Selfish old me. Going to the quilting club for the first time in seven years all by myself.

The really bad part is that I don't have anybody to talk to about this. I can't tell Diana because that would be disloyal. Besides, she'd tell Josh and then everybody would be taking sides. I certainly can't talk to Patsy because the last time we disagreed over a man we split up and didn't see each other for a year. And I'm not fixing to let that happen again.

Josh was two when we had our big fight. Not that we hadn't had small disagreements. You can't live with somebody and a baby in three rooms and not get on each other's nerves, even if that somebody is your best friend.

In spite of my protests that Lulu's was no place for a mother, Patsy was singing and waiting tables there again.

"I'm not going to live off you forever," she said. "Besides, I'll be bringing home a second paycheck. Eventually we can get a bigger place."

I never should have let her talk me into that arrangement, but I did, and everything was going along fine until she brought home more than a paycheck.

One morning I got up to make coffee, and there he was sprawled across the couch. Patsy heard my yelp and came running.

"This is Bob." She announced him in an offhand way as if having a man on the sofa was an ordinary occurrence, which was as far from the truth as you can get. We'd hardly even talked about men, let alone dated one, since I came to New Orleans.

Bob sat up and ran his hand through his already bushed-out hair. "Uh…I guess I'd better be going."

When he pushed back the quilt and headed to the door, I was happy to see he still had his pants on.

"Patsy, what in the world's going on here?"

"Bob's the bartender at Lulu's. He's left his wife and needed a place to stay. He came home with me last night to talk, that's all. We lost track of time and he stayed."

"Just don't let it happen again."

"Who made you boss?"

"Look, all I'm saying is that we have enough on our plates right now without adding complications."

Patsy didn't argue anymore, and for the next two weeks she was unusually quiet and docile—a dead giveaway of trouble brewing if I had been paying attention. But I wasn't. I was giving exams.

Then one day I came home and found a note: "I wasn't born to be a millstone. Don't worry about Josh. I'd take on Hannibal and his whole damn army of war elephants for my son."

Do you know how a place feels after the people you love get in their banged-up old Chevrolet and drive away? Like a beating heart, suddenly stilled. Like a rose stripped of fragrance. Like a forest without birdsong.

I'll never risk that again.

## CHAPTER 5

*Patsy*

From: "Miss Sass" patsyleslie@hotmail.com
To: "The Lady" louisejernigan@yahoo.com
Sent: Thursday, August 17, 7:00 a.m.
Subject: THE DATE!
I don't know if I'm coming or going. I don't know how I'll keep my mind on work today. Do you think the Lycra skirt is a little over the top or should I stick with something more conservative? My yellow linen pants suit? Hells bells, I've turned into a basket case full of cellulite.
Gotta run! I'll e-mail you when I get home tonight with FULL DETAILS!
XOXO
Patsy, running around like a chicken with her head cut off

P.S. About your advice re: my legs... You think Gorilla Glue would do the trick?

Louise must be sitting at her computer waiting, because her reply's not long coming.

From: "The Lady" louisejernigan@yahoo.com
To: "Miss Sass" patsyleslie@hotmail.com
Sent: Thursday, August 17, 7:04 a.m.
Subject: Re: THE DATE!
You don't need Gorilla Glue. Just pretend you're me.
XOXO, right back at you
Louise

I'm not about to let her have the last word.

From: "Miss Sass" patsyleslie@hotmail.com
To: "The Lady" louisejernigan@yahoo.com
Sent: Thursday, August 17, 7:06 a.m.
Subject: Not a chance!
You tend to your legs and I'll tend to mine!
XOXOX
Patsy, off to another scintillating day with Herbert

On the way to work I nearly run the stop sign on the corner of Robins and Jefferson, so I make myself take deep breaths and slow down. Nothing turns a man off like an overeager woman. And I'm not fixing to turn off Harry Thompson.

What I'm fixing to do is turn him on.

I had expected something a bit more exotic than the Pickle Barrel in Amory, but it turns out that Harry's from California and still enamored of all things "Deep South," which explains his desire for fried catfish and hush puppies.

It also turns out my Lycra and heels are way over the top, but when Harry runs his hand up my thigh, who cares if everybody else is in blue jeans and denim shorts and flip-flops.

And for your information, I'm wearing the black lace panties, too. Louise or no Louise. If I don't have enough sense at my age to handle my peach blossom, I never will.

Besides, I learned a thing or two at LuLu's. How to judge men, for one. Telling the good ones from the bad ones was a matter of self-preservation in the French Quarter.

That skill comes in handy when Harry wants to take me to his place after dinner.

"Not tonight."

I'm not fixing to let him think I'm easy. In spite of all my big talk about my motor being revved and my libido not being dead, it's not sex I have on my mind. Well, I take that back. Of course I have sex on my mind. I'm a red-blooded woman still in her prime.

But what nobody knows—except Louise—is that I've been lonely ever since Rocky died, not the loneliness you feel from living by yourself but a gut-deep longing for your heart's other half.

Oh, I've covered it up fine all these years. Bill never knew. He was a good man—a little too bossy, much too conservative and a bit judgmental—but still, a good man.

And loneliness is not something you talk about with your son. You want to be perfect in a son's eyes, a strong, independent woman who has no intention of turning whiny and clingy and needy.

Sure, Harry rings my chimes and I'd climb in bed with him in a heartbeat if I wanted a casual fling. But I don't. What I want is another Rocky Delgado. I want a hero who will put big, protective arms around me and love me till the day I die.

It's too soon to tell, but I have a feeling Harry could turn out to be that guy.

When we return to my place I do allow him to kiss me, and I'm here to tell you I haven't been kissed like that since high school. Mouths wide open and lots of tongue. The tenderness will come in time. I'm certain.

"I want to see you again, Patsy. Sunday?"

I feel only a little twinge of guilt when I say, "Yes." There'll be plenty more Sunday dinners. Besides, the kids are in Memphis.

"Do you like boating? I thought we could drive up to Pickwick Lake."

Thank God I have a tan. Now, if I can grow Julia Roberts's legs overnight, I'll be cooking.

"That would be great." Now that my first date in years is over, I'm itching to go inside and e-mail Louise.

"I want you all to myself, Patsy." He cups my face the way Rocky used to, and I swear at that moment I'd run all the way to the North Pole and back if he'd ask me. "I'd like to keep what we have just between the two of us. Our private little heaven. Don't you agree?"

"Of course."

There goes my tell-all e-mail session with Louise. Still, what Harry's saying makes sense. What goes on between a man and a woman ought to be kept private.

I'm sure Louise will agree. We were just high school kids when I was telling her every detail of my courtship with Rocky. We're not kids anymore. Not by several decades.

She'll probably even quote one of those poets she's so fond of. Emily Dickenson. The verse about showing out in public like a frog.

See. In spite of the fact that I never went to college, I'm nobody's fool.

*Louise*

Driving to quilting club alone, I feel as if I've forgotten something important. My purse. (It's right there on the seat.) My teeth. (I check in the rearview mirror to see if I forgot to brush and there's a piece of lettuce caught in the front.) My mind. (Hello, hello, is anybody home?)

I turn on the radio to fill the silence, make sure I pay attention to red lights and arrive fifteen minutes early at Betty Lynn Jones's house.

She meets me at the door with only one eye made-up.

"My goodness! Where's Patsy?"

"She couldn't come tonight."

"Sick?"

"No. She had other plans."

"A man?"

Well…here I am still standing in the doorway like a delivery boy while Betty Lynn pumps me for information. In the first place, I'd never betray Patsy, and in the second, when somebody does me this way I ruffle up like a flounced petticoat in a forty-mile-an-hour gale.

"I didn't ask. May I come in? It's hot out here."

"Oh…of course. Just make yourself at home. I'll only be a minute."

Betty Lynn's the kind of person who matches everything in her house. Green pillow on the green-and-tan striped sofa, which picks up the green accents in her rug and the green geometric pattern of her curtains. I clash. My purple dress stands out like a bruise in this color-coordinated room.

*Entertainment Weekly*, *People* and *Tinsel Town Tell-All* are stacked neatly in a green laminated basket at my feet. I flip through all three. How long does it take to put mascara on one eye?

If Patsy were here, she's have some smart remark. If you want to know the truth, if Patsy were here we wouldn't even *be* here. I'd be standing at my door with my purse waiting for her to finish drinking one last sip of Diet Pepsi before she dashed out her door.

I feel lost.

Betty Lynn doesn't come back until Mary Jo Barton arrives. That's okay with me. It gives me more time to think up reasons for Patsy's absence.

Mary Jo plops down beside me with her tote bag of quilting squares.

"I heard Patsy met a man at the bank," she says.

Geez. Patsy always said she was nosy, but I didn't believe her.

"I'm sure Patsy sees new customers every day at the bank. Did we come here to quilt or what?"

Patsy could have pulled that remark off, but Mary Jo stares at me as if I've said she needs dental work and a face-lift.

"Quilting's more fun if you gossip," Betty Lynn says, and we all end up laughing.

I feel rescued. It's these small mercies that keep us going.

The evening seems longer than usual, and by the time I get home I'm worn out. Maybe I need to cut back on nighttime activities. Lord, I feel as old as Aunt Charlotte.

It's all I can do to drag myself to the computer. I flip the switch, then stare at Patsy's e-mail, puzzled and more than a little irritated. After all, who kept her out of the gossip mill tonight at quilting club?

If Patsy were here she'd say I'm being overly dramatic and too sensitive. But, of course, she's not here. She's tucked in her bed...by herself, I hope, but how am I to know? Certainly not by this puny, secretive e-mail.

From: "Miss Sass" patsyleslie@hotmail.com
To: "The Lady" louisejernigan@yahoo.com
Sent: Thursday, August 17, 10:30 p.m.
Subject: My date with Harry
We had a catfish dinner at the Pickle Barrel in Amory. Harry's a very nice man. I'm going out with him again on Sunday. I hope you don't mind. That means I'll be missing our usual Sunday dinner, but there will always be more!
Hugs,
Patsy

It's not Sunday dinner I mind. Well, I do, really, but that's just plain silly. It's impossible for anybody to keep a standing date year after year without ever missing a single one. Emergencies arise. People get the flu. Tomcats get in fights and have to be rushed to the vet. Teachers' conferences in Texas intervene.

Still…I've never stood her up for a man. Why

couldn't she tell him she'd meet him after dinner? Why didn't she just invite him along?

I suddenly have a vision of myself jumping into a lifeboat expecting Patsy to jump in right after me only to discover she's hailed the Coast Guard and sailed off without me.

The really awful truth about this note is that it tells me nothing about Harry. He's *nice?* What in the world does that mean? He's nice because he has all his own teeth? He's nice because he doesn't belch in public? He's nice because he excused himself before he went to the toilet?

Oh, I'm on a roll here. Just plain mean-spirited. If I didn't know better, I'd say I was jealous. But of course, I'm not. Roy was enough man to last a lifetime.

Still…I feel so left out, so completely alone. How could Patsy do this to me? We've always told each other everything.

The e-mail is sitting there, accusing me. Well, I don't know what to say. How can I answer? But if I don't, Patsy will think I'm sick. Or worse… upset.

From: "The Lady" louisejernigan@yahoo.com
To: "Miss Sass" patsyleslie@hotmail.com
Sent: Thursday, August 17, 10:45 p.m.
Subject: Re: My date with Harry
I'm glad you had a nice evening. Enjoy your
Sunday date, and don't worry about me.
Love,
Louise


I study the screen as if world peace hinges on
my reply. Maybe I ought to take the don't-worry-
about-me part out. When somebody says, Don't
worry about me, it's usually said in a whiny voice
that means, You'd better worry about me because
you've gone off and abandoned me and I'm feeling
very sorry for myself.

I delete don't worry about me. Now the note is
too short. Curt sounding. Like I'm mad. Which,
of course, I'm not.

Oh, for Pete's sake!

I get up and stomp around the room, straight-
ening the bookshelves, rearranging the framed
photographs of Josh and Diana, of Patsy and me.

The darned computer sounds like somebody breathing. I want to stomp it flat.

Good heavens, I'm turning into a woman who needs Prozac. What I need is tea. With lots of sugar and cream.

Sitting at the kitchen table soothing myself with sugar and cream, I think about the small mercies and tender caring of friendship. Being friends is not being in each other's pockets every day; it's loving and supporting each other even when you're apart, no matter what the circumstances.

If I'm going to call myself Patsy's friend, then I'd better act like one.

Taking my tea with me, I sit down at the computer, delete the entire message, including the To and From, and start all over.

From: "The Lady" louisejernigan@yahoo.com
To: "Miss Sass" patsyleslie@hotmail.com
Sent: Thursday, August 17, 10:55 p.m.
Subject: Re: My date with Harry
Hey, girlfriend! The Pickle Barrel is a great place to relax and have fun. Remember that time we placed a double order of fried pickles and made

ourselves sick because neither of us likes to waste food and we both hate to pay for something and then throw it out? Anyhow, I'm glad you enjoyed your date with Harry. And I really mean that. You deserve a good time.

Much love,

Louise

*There*. That's better. I press send then finish my tea and watch the tail end of *From Here to Eternity*, which gives me a good excuse to cry.

Afterward I climb in bed and wrap my arms around myself, grateful for this—the soft shirt that once lay against Roy's olive skin enfolding me in memories.

From: "Miss Sass" patsyleslie@hotmail.com
To: "The Lady" louisejernigan@yahoo.com
Sent: Friday, August 18, 7:00 a.m.
Subject: King Kong
I put King Kong on the screened-in back porch last night, and he went on a tear. Ripped every one of my potted petunias to shreds.
Gotta run. Fridays are always hectic.

Do you want to go to the movies tonight? I'm dying to see that new one with George Clooney.
XOXOX
Patsy, pissed at her cat


From: "The Lady" louisejernigan@yahoo.com
To: "Miss Sass" patsyleslie@hotmail.com
Sent: Friday, August 18, 7:05 a.m.
Subject: Re: King Kong
If you'd have that cat neutered he wouldn't be so destructive.
Can't go to the movies tonight. Got a board meeting of Friends of the Library. We're gearing up for our fall book sale. How about tomorrow? Maybe we could shop for baby clothes, have lunch, then drool over Clooney.
Much love,
Louise, glad Kong is not my cat


From: "Miss Sass" patsyleslie@hotmail.com
To: "The Lady" louisejernigan@yahoo.com
Sent: Friday, August 18, 7:08 a.m.
Subject: Re: King Kong
Can't go. Gotta get this hair chopped, fluffed,

oiled, tortured, colored and RESCUED. Probably take most of the day.

Want to come?

XOXOX

Patsy, still pissed at her cat, but not THAT pissed

From: "The Lady" louisejernigan@yahoo.com
To: "Miss Sass" patsyleslie@hotmail.com
Sent: Friday, August 18, 7:10 a.m.
Subject: Re: King Kong
Sorry. I have to be at the library all day Saturday sorting books for the Friends' sale.

Hugs,

Louise, still glad Kong's not my cat

From: "Miss Sass" patsyleslie@hotmail.com
To: "The Lady" louisejernigan@yahoo.com
Sent: Friday, August 18, 7:12 a.m.
Subject: Re: King Kong
Okay. Have fun. Gotta run. Herbert will be in a snit if I'm late.

Later.

XOXOX

P, thinking about swapping Kong for a nice, docile dog that won't shed

## CHAPTER 6

*Louise*

**It's** Sunday evening. Here's my whirlwind day so far: sitting on the fifth pew at First Methodist trying to pay attention to a sermon about Jonah and the whale (me, if I don't stop eating so much butter) when I was worried about Sodom and Gomorroh (Patsy with her shady stranger), then taking a pot of beef stew to the farm and refereeing a fight between Aunt Charlotte and Uncle Bradley about the John Deere keys (what else!).

Now I'm home watching reruns of *The Golden Girls* while Patsy's still at Pickwick with Harry doing Lord-knows-what. It doesn't take a Philadelphia lawyer to figure it out.

Early this morning when she pranced in here,

her newly disheveled hair was a dead giveaway. Besides that, she was wearing sling-back high heels (for the lake, no less!) and too much mascara. She looked like a woman fixing to have sex.

"How do you like my hair?"

"It makes you look ten years younger."

And that's the truth. The color was over the top (platinum blond), the style was straight out of Hollywood (tousled with hair hanging in the eyes), and the cut was teenager-looking (too short to put in a French twist), but she looked more "pure Patsy" than I've seen her since she married Rocky Delgado.

"You really think so?" she asked.

"I really think so. You look great."

"Good. Wish me luck."

"For what?"

"This is the second date, Louise. I'm just liable to turn loose and party."

"You be careful, that's all."

"You worry too much."

I know I do. It's after ten and I haven't heard a car come back into her driveway. Getting out of my comfortable recliner, I pull back my den curtains. Through the hedge I can see that her porch light's on and that's all.

If I call her cell phone to see about her, I'm liable to interrupt something, so I make myself sit down and watch *The Golden Girls*. But even they are talking about sex. Blanche is on the prowl and Dorothy is sleeping with Stanley. Again.

For Pete's sake. These women are my age. Shouldn't they be quilting? Something must be wrong with me.

I switch over to HBO but everywhere I look somebody's seducing somebody else. Finally I give up and go in the kitchen to pop some corn. I'll melt real butter for the top. Shoot, I'll go whole hog and make peanut butter popcorn.

While the corn's still popping I see headlights in Patsy's driveway and breathe a sigh of relief. Now I can concentrate on the topping: bring a half cup of sugar and a half cup of corn syrup to a boil, add a half cup of peanut butter and one teaspoonful of vanilla.

Stirring this decadent brew, I glance toward the window, expecting the car to pull back out, but it never does. A few of Patsy's lights pop on, then her house is dark again.

Finally I pour the popcorn in a bowl, add the topping then go to my computer to check my e-mail.

There are no messages tonight. Patsy has more exciting things to do than e-chat with me.

I shut off the computer, put on purple pajamas, then eat sitting in the middle of my bed. And I don't give a flip if I get sticky kernels on the sheets and my figure's starting to resemble a gourd-necked squash.

*Patsy*

I think I have died and gone to Tahiti. The next thing you know I'm going to be prancing around on top of my bed tossing off a coconut-shell bra.

*Honey, hush!* Harry ought to have that thing bronzed and hung on a plaque. A big plaque.

I'm here to tell you, he was worth waiting for. If you call Thursday to Sunday waiting.

He broke a sweat, and so did I. When we pull apart there's this *sound*, like somebody plunging the toilet. I'm glad I'm not the kind of woman who minds. This is not the movies where everybody is long-limbed and golden: this is real life where bellies bulge and skin sags and important body parts have lost their fight with gravity. This is the truth, where minds are more important than bodies and spirits are more significant than age.

"Hmmm," Harry murmurs.

I'm getting ready to say, That's just what I was thinking, when Harry makes the humming sound again. He's not expressing pleasure, but clearing his throat. I've saved myself a potload of embarrassment by keeping my mouth shut.

A good lesson if I'll learn it.

I smooth the wrinkled sheets, then stretch in what I hope is a sexy fashion. The best part's coming up, the part where he climbs back into bed and we cuddle close and fall asleep in each other's arms.

Instead, Harry reaches for his pants.

"Do you want something to drink?" I ask. "Something to eat?"

"I've got to go, babe. Tomorrow's a busy day. See you Tuesday? Around eight?"

"Great."

There goes bridge club. I grab my robe, then switch on lights. A calculated reversal.

A sneak peek in the mirror shows that my hair held up well even if my face didn't. Mascara's smudged down one cheek. I whirl around and try to wipe it off before he notices.

I needn't have bothered. When I turn back he's standing in front of my dresser holding framed photos of the kids' wedding picture and Louise and me in Hawaii.

"Who's this?"

"My son, Josh, and my daughter-in-law, Diana. The other is my best friend, Louise Jernigan."

"Great-looking kids."

"Thanks."

"Your friend looks like a nice lady."

"She's a real lady. One of the few I know."

"What does she do?"

"She's an English teacher at Tupelo High and secretary of Friends of the Library. There's nothing she can't do."

"Smart, huh?"

"Very. I'm lucky. I know how to pick friends."

Harry sets the photographs down, comes over and hugs me. "I hope I'm one of them, toots."

I tell him yes then walk him to the door, keeping my mouth shut because I don't want to jeopardize a relationship that might turn into the same kind of magic I had with Rocky. There'll be time enough to tell him I don't like to be called "toots" and "babe."

I stand in the doorway watching until his lights disappear into the darkness, then go back inside, take a picture of Rocky out of the top drawer of the bedside table and sit there blinking back tears, Patsy Delgado, trapped in the middle of her very own *Love Story*, idolizing the dead.

From: "Miss Sass" patsyleslie@hotmail.com
To: "The Lady" louisejernigan@yahoo.com
Sent: Monday, August 21, 7:00 a.m.
Subject: Everything
Had a great time at the lake. How was Sunday dinner?
XOXXO
P, still smiling

From: "The Lady" louisejernigan@yahoo.com
To: "Miss Sass" patsyleslie@hotmail.com
Sent: Monday, August 21, 7:10 a.m.
Subject: Re: Everything
I'm glad you had a good time. Sunday was fine. I
made a pot of soup for Aunt Charlotte and Uncle
Bradley and cleaned closets. The kids got back from
Memphis around three and stopped by. They asked
where you were. Haven't you told Josh about Harry?
I've got to run. Today's the first day of school. I
don't want to keep my eager students waiting. ?
Hugs,
Louise

From: "Miss Sass" patsyleslie@hotmail.com
To: "The Lady" louisejernigan@yahoo.com
Sent: Monday, August 21, 6:00 p.m.
Subject: Harry and the kids
Jeez, Louise! I worried all day about what you told
the kids about Harry. NO, I haven't told Josh yet.
I'm trying to decide what to tell. I don't know yet
if Harry's a keeper, and if he's not, why get the kids
in on it? You know how Josh is. Overprotective.
He keeps calling my cell. I left a generic hi-there-
how-are-you message on his cell last night when

I knew he'd be at Wellness Center working out. Lord, he's so predictable.

XOXXO

Patsy, on pins and needles


From: "The Lady" louisejernigan@yahoo.com
To: "Miss Sass" patsyleslie@hotmail.com
Sent: Monday, August 21, 9:00 p.m.
Subject: Re: Harry and the kids

I had a ton of things to do after school today. As always, the students both energize me and wear me out. Lord, all those expectations and person-alities!

How could you even think I'd tell your secrets? All I said was, "She's going in so many directions these days I can't keep up with her." That satis-fied Josh and Diana, but you'd better gird yourself for Mary Jo Barton tomorrow night at bridge. She's heard about Harry from the bank, and her gossip pump is primed.

Hugs,

Louise, getting ready to put her feet up

P.S. Don't you think telling the kids you have a new male friend would be easier than all this pussy-footing around?

From: "Miss Sass" patsyleslie@hotmail.com
To: "The Lady" louisejernigan@yahoo.com
Sent: Monday, August 21, 9:10 p.m.
Subject: Re: Harry and the kids

I might tell tomorrow, but I'm thinking of waiting till Sunday dinner so you'll be there to lend moral support. Plus, you always know what to say.

Oh…I forgot to tell you…I'm going out with Harry tomorrow night. I guess I'd better call Mary Jo to get a fourth. Thanks for warning me that she knows. She'll ask a million questions. What can I tell her?

XOXOX

Patsy, with her tail in a crack—as usual

P.S. I can't go to quilting Thursday, either. Sorry. Laura Lee at the bank is giving Herbert a birthday dinner at Las Margaritas. I don't dare stay home. I'm in enough trouble with that old battle ax already!

From: "The Lady" louisejernigan@yahoo.com
To: "Miss Sass" patsyleslie@hotmail.com
Sent: Monday, August 21, 9:15 p.m.
Subject: Re: Harry and the kids

Tell Mary Jo the same thing I told the kids—you're

going in so many directions you can't even keep
tabs on yourself.
Love,
Louise, calling it a night

*Louise*

I'm not calling it a night; I'm calling Mary Jo
to tell her I won't be at bridge club and Betty Lynn
to say I'm can't come to quilting. If Patsy thinks
I'm going to endure the third-degree on her
account, she's sadly mistaken.

Of course, I don't know a thing about Harry,
but Mary Jo and Betty Lynn won't believe that,
especially Mary Jo. She'll keep prodding till I get
a headache, and I'm too smart to deliberately
open myself up to pain and suffering. Even on
Patsy's behalf.

It might be different if she'd told me things, but
*no*, she had to go off and do stuff she won't even
tell her own children.

Well, *okay*, I admit it. Self-righteous indignation is unbecoming, especially in a friend. Before

I call Mary Jo I make myself a quick cup of tea (meaning I zap the water in the microwave, usually against my principles), then add cream and sugar. I even splurge, add a dash of cinnamon, a dollop of vanilla—and a little extra cream.

This calming brew works miracles, and I tell myself to buck up.

But change is hard, so I don't chastise myself too much. Instead I dive into the comfort of real cream, take a deep breath and pick up the phone.

*Patsy*

Tuesday night Harry shows up in a different vehicle, a big old Dodge Ram pickup Rocky would have called a bad-boy, kick-ass truck. But don't get me started down that road or I'll start paying attention to Harry's flaws. For one thing, he's not tender like Rocky.

Basic character doesn't change, so that means he never will hold me close and call me "precious," never fall asleep in the middle of the afternoon stretched across the bed with his lips on mine. But I'm learning to live with it. What choice do I have?

Face it, women my age aren't going to find heroes lined up outside our doors. The good ones are usually taken, either moving gracefully into the golden years with a woman they still adore after thirty years, or sticking it out with a woman they long ago stopped loving because staying is easier (and less expensive) than leaving.

After being called "toots" and "babe," I have the sneaking suspicion I'm like that old country-and-western song, looking for love in all the wrong places. Still, it's too early to tell, and I'm having a good time.

Joy matters. Too many people just give up and go around with sour expressions and joyless attitudes. Not me. I plan to live my life.

Then why do I go every day to a job I hate?

I won't spoil the evening by thinking about that. Instead, I ask Harry, "Did you trade cars? My black lace goes much better with a Corvette than a Dodge pickup."

"No. The 'Vette's in my garage. Cars are my

weakness." When he helps me into his truck he runs his hand up my leg, and let me tell you, my black lace is not wasted.

"Cars and you," he adds.

This is going to be another five-star date. I can already tell.

When we go past Louise's I let my libido idle long enough to see if she's already at bridge, but her car's still in the driveway. What if she's sick, and here I am squirting off to have a big time?

"I hope you don't mind," I tell Harry, then jerk out my cell phone and punch in her number without waiting to see whether he does or not.

"Louise? Where are you?"

"At home. Why?"

"Are you sick?"

"No, but I told Mary Jo I was."

"With what?"

"I said I was coming down with a virus."

"Good. I did, too. Maybe she'll think it's a bug that's going around. Gotta run. Love you."

After I hang up, Harry asks, "Is she okay?"

I tell him yes, although I'm not sure. Louise

didn't sound like herself. I guess I wouldn't sound like myself, either, if my best friend had abandoned me three times to be with a man.

But I can't believe anything could ever damage or destroy our friendship, not after we survived our own private Battle of New Orleans.

Lord, nobody will ever know how alone I felt back then, driving off without Louise. I almost turned around in Slidell and went back, but when I got to thinking about that phone call she'd had the day before, I knew the best thing I could do was keep on going.

I was brushing my teeth, getting ready for work at LuLu's when the phone rang.

Louise answered and I heard only her end of the conversation. "No, I can't…I'm sorry, I can't go Friday night either…. No, Saturday is not good for me. Listen, James, don't take this personally, but right now is not a good time for me to see anybody."

I never said a word to her about that phone call, but let me tell you, I wasn't fixing to let Louise sacrifice her whole life for Josh and me.

Discussing it with her was out of the question.

She'd still be arguing. I just packed up Josh and left. I knew she'd think it was over that big fight we had about the bartender, and that suited my purposes fine. I had to get her good and mad so she'd go on with her life.

Now Harry says, "Is the Pontotoc Inn fine with you?"

"Sure."

Sex first. Well, that suits me fine. I like a man who has his priorities straight.

But it turns out that all he wants at the Pontotoc Inn is spaghetti.

"I hope you don't mind calling it a night early," he says after dinner, and it's all I can do to get my libido settled back down.

Italian food and Italian studs just go together, and although Harry's not foreign, I figured he was setting the stage for a night where my black lace would end up on the lampshade and I'd end up in hog heaven.

"That's fine," I say.

"Sorry to disappoint you, toots." I let that slide. "How about another Sunday date?"

I tell him no.

Fortunately he's understanding about the traditional dinner with the kids, intrigued that Louise and I are in-laws, and hot for another date next Tuesday.

What can I say? Bridge takes a back seat to sex, or even the possibility thereof.

When I get home, I send Louise an e-mail.

From: "Miss Sass" patsyleslie@hotmail.com
To: "The Lady" louisejernigan@yahoo.com
Sent: Tuesday, August 22, 11:00 p.m.
Subject: You
I'm worried about you. You're probably not up this late, but as soon as you get this e-mail, call me. I don't care what time it is.
XOXO
Patsy, your best friend and don't you forget it!

I've got my makeup off and I'm standing in the bathroom with the toothbrush in my mouth when my phone rings a few minutes later.

"Ummlo."

"Patsy? You said call."

"Yust ah minit." I race into the bathroom and

spit, then grab the phone. "I was brushing my teeth. What are you doing up so late?"

"Couldn't sleep, that's all."

"Are you sure that's all. Lately you've seemed awfully…I don't know…depressed."

"I'm tired."

"That's one of the signs."

"Who made you the expert? You're never depressed. I wish I could be more like you," she said.

"No, you don't. You have a job you love, a wonderful marriage to remember and a grandbaby on the way. *I'm* batting one out of three."

Listen to me, running on about my own problems. "So what's really eating you, Gilbert Grape?"

Louise giggles, and I plop on my bed, proud of myself.

"Guess who got picked for the teacher grant? William Butler."

"That old windbag?"

"Exactly. He's dry, he never varies from the book, he grades as if math is the only subject worth considering, and the kids dislike him."

"No wonder you're depressed. Do you want

me to come over with a bottle of wine so we can get drunk?"

"I have to work tomorrow and so do you."

"We could lie again. Say we had a virus."

"We'd better not...Patsy, how are you? Is everything working out well with Harry?"

"Great." Oh, I feel like a toad, not telling her a few details. Nothing too personal, just enough so we can savor this experience together. "Harry has a good sense of humor. We laugh a lot, and he's not half-bad in the sack. But I guess you already figured out that we're sleeping together."

"I wouldn't call it that."

"Neither would I, girlfriend!"

I'm glad I sent the e-mail, and even happier that I could leave her laughing. When I turn out the lights and snuggle under the sheet, I feel like a better person. Maybe there's hope for me, after all.

## CHAPTER 7

*Louise*

**The** last thing I expected to see in my classroom so soon after the start of school was a parent, especially a father. Even though he looks pleasant and mannerly—an attractive dark-haired man in a business suit—I brace myself. Parents who don't call ahead for appointments usually spell trouble.

"May I help you?"

"Yes. Louise? Louise Jernigan?" I nod, and he says, "I'm sorry to take you by surprise, but I have a set of law books I want to donate to the Friends of the Library for their book sale, and I was told you're the person to see."

Relief makes me effusive. "Of course! We'd be delighted to have your books. How thoughtful of you to take time from your schedule to come by. I know how busy lawyers are."

"The books belonged to my father. I'm afraid I'm nothing more than a lowly engineer."

"You do yourself an injustice. Civic-minded people get a high rating from me." If I didn't know better I'd say I was flirting, which is ridiculous at my age. Still, this is an intriguing man. Well, a stranger really. "I'm sorry, I didn't catch your name."

"Wayne Thompson. I wonder if you could meet me at the library this evening, show me where to take the books."

"It's the least I can do."

"Great. Is six good for you?"

"Perfect."

I sound like June Cleaver on *Leave It to Beaver*. After Wayne leaves I waste five minutes standing at my desk doing nothing except wondering why I didn't say "Great," or "See you then." Anything except "Perfect." Lord, he must have thought I'm a deprived older woman who viewed him as a last chance at sex. And in the library, no less.

"Mrs. Jernigan?"

I jump as if my student has metamorphosed into Aunt Charlotte and poked me with a cattle prod. "Yes, Janice. What is it?"

"I was wondering if I have to read that whole *Prince of Tides* thing or if I can just rent the movie."

"You have to read the book. And, Janice…I'll know if you didn't."

This is the kind of conversation that would depress me if I let it. Each fall I have a room full of Janices who hate to read.

My challenge is to teach them not only to use correct grammar and write a complete sentence, but also to love the written word. How can they ever appreciate beauty and understand passion if they don't thrill to great literary works such as Edna St. Vincent Millay's "Journey."

When the final bell rings my mind is still on the beauty of Millay's poem. It's certainly not on my feet, because I stumble over a large piece of gravel in the parking lot.

In one of those slow-motion moments, I see myself smashing into the pavement, breaking my cheekbone, knocking out a tooth and splintering one leg. The next crazy thing I see is Wayne standing in the library entrance watching a gray-haired, beat-up old cripple hobble his way.

I regain my balance against the side of my car and suffer nothing more than a throbbing ankle and the uncomfortable feeling that I'm headed down a slippery slope toward trouble. How ridiculous to be thinking about a man during a moment of crisis, instead of something sensible. Taking out the garbage, for instance. That would be hard to do on a crutch. So would bending over to get the morning paper or standing on a stepstool to reach the bug spray when you find ants in the kitchen.

You have to think about these things when you live alone.

I settle into the driver's seat, catch my breath and dial Diana at the clinic.

"Hon, can I drive by and let you take a look at my ankle. I think I might have fractured it."

I'm hiked up on Diana's examining table and she's fixing to put an ugly elastic bandage around my ankle. That lets out cute wedge-heeled sandals and a little extra sizzle in the hips. Not that I plan to flaunt myself around in front of Wayne Thompson just because he smelled like Irish Spring (Roy's favorite soap). Still, I wanted to be moderately alluring, the kind of woman who mystifies and intrigues instead of the kind who carries samples of lip gloss she never uses in her purse just because it's free.

"Mom, did you hear me?"

"What?"

"I said stay off it as much as possible, put your feet up tonight to help reduce the swelling."

"Well…"

"Well what?"

"I have a date. Sort of."

"What do you mean, sort of? Either you do or you don't."

I tell her about Wayne, leaving out the details I want to keep to myself. The way his hair falls across his forehead. His really nice smile. Little things you notice when you meet a man who jolts you into consciousness of your own femininity.

"Good for you, Mom. Wear something cute."

"I don't have anything cute. Besides, it's not a date."

She walks to the door and calls for Josh. When he strides into the room, I see the little boy who loved fire trucks and Big Bird and kites on windy days. I'm struck by the swift passage of time and how every choice we make shapes not only who we are but the lives of those we touch.

"Hey, Mama Two." He has called me this since he was eleven months old and learned to talk.

Josh kisses me on the cheek, and I know that somewhere inside this big, handsome, successful young man is the intrepid toddler who ventured from Patsy's grasp to mine, walking weeks before the child-care manuals said he should. Somewhere inside is the little boy who considered the blond-haired cherub next door his personal charge and gave up afternoons of frog catching and tree climbing to play peek-a-boo with Diana.

"Check out her ankle, Josh. I think it's just sprained."

"What have you been doing?" He gently tests

my range of motion. "Playing football with some of your students?"

"I'm not that brave."

"Don't let Mama hear you say that." He nods to Diana and she starts wrapping my ankle. "What's she up to?"

"I haven't seen much of her since school started."

He laughs. "I know better than to ask one of you to rat on the other. Are you coming to our house for lunch Sunday?"

"I wouldn't miss it."

Driving home I'm thinking, This is enough, this wonderful daughter and son-in-law, this life-long friendship that feels as if I have a sister, this pleasant routine filled with books and students and quilting and hot tea with cream.

But is it? Now that I have a glimmer of hope for a bit more, I don't know. I don't know anything anymore.

From: "The Lady" louisejernigan@yahoo.com
To: "Miss Sass" patsyleslie@hotmail.com
Sent: Wednesday, August 23, 7:00 p.m.

Subject: Wayne
I'll bet you're flabbergasted at my subject.
Actually, so am I. I met a man!

I stop typing and stare at the exclamation point
as if it's a new kind of virus that has invaded my
home. Geez, since when do I do anything that
requires exclamation points to explain?

My hand is on the delete key, when I say,
"What the heck, just let her rip."

He donated a trunkful of really fine law books to the
Friends, and after we finished unloading them at
the library, he asked me for a date. A real one, if you
can believe that. I'm going to dinner tomorrow
night with a great-looking engineer named Wayne,
and for the first time in four years I feel like a woman.
XOXO
Louise, excited and scared to death!!!

From: "Miss Sass" patsyleslie@hotmail.com
To: "The Lady" louisejernigan@yahoo.com
Sent: Wednesday, August 23, 7:15 p.m.
Subject: Re: Wayne

Here I was sitting at home by myself eating a frozen chicken pot pie (you know me, I'm too lazy to cook) and picturing you at some dull old teacher's meeting while you're out kicking the traces (finally!!!!!) and kicking up your heels.

Listen, don't you dare wear your old school-marm duds tomorrow night. Wear something sexy. I'll lend you my Lycra skirt. It sure worked for me! ? Or we can go shopping. If we hurry we can get to the mall and have an hour before the stores close.

What do you say?

XOXOX

Patsy, who says stop being scared and turn Tilly loose, girlfriend!

P.S. I'm driving!


From: "The Lady" louisejernigan@yahoo.com
To: "Miss Sass" patsyleslie@hotmail.com
Sent: Wednesday, August 23, 7:20 p.m.
Subject: Shopping

Meet me in my driveway in five minutes.

XOXOX

Louise, keeping her legs together and a tight hold on Tilly

*Patsy*

Here she comes in a pair of unstylish slacks I'd be embarrassed to give to Goodwill.

"Jeez, Louise! What happened to your leg?"

"It's just a sprained ankle."

"Shoot, that lets out red high heels."

"I wasn't planning on red high heels, just something a little flashier than sneakers."

"Oh, hell, Louise. Live large."

After she settles in, I peel out toward the mall, making up for lost time. I swear, it takes her forever to get into a car. She acts like she's trying to figure out the perfect, most ladylike way. Just plop your butt on the seat, find Willie Nelson or Tim McGraw on the radio and boogie on down the road, that's my motto.

When we get to the mall she heads toward the old fuddy-duddy section of Parisian's like somebody perfectly satisfied to drift into old age. I'm not fixing to drift myself, or let her either if I can help it, so I yank her off toward better dresses, snatch summer sweaters featuring Lycra and march her toward the dressing rooms.

"I don't know about these," she protests.

"I do. Put one on."

"Lord…" She turns this way and that in a rose-colored sweater that puts a little color in her cheeks and knocks twenty years off her age. "I look like somebody launching a couple of ballistic missiles."

"If you point them in the right direction, you're liable to land on the moon. Flaunt it, Louise."

"In front of my students?"

"Why not? Just because you're gray, doesn't mean you're dead. I believe in grabbing opportunity while you can still hear it knocking."

"I've never heard sex called opportunity."

"Shut up and pay for the sweater, Louise. I want to get you some red lipstick before they run us out of the store."

I couldn't talk her into red, but she did settle on a rich rose that will do the trick if she'll loosen up.

After we get in the car to head home, she gets too quiet over there on the passenger side. A bad sign.

"You're not sitting there thinking you're fixing to betray Roy, are you?"

"How did you know?"

"I know you. That's all."

Louise is the one who can talk a person out of these moods, not me. Still, I've got to try. I don't believe in letting your best friend crawl in a cave and post a Keep Out sign on the front.

Listen, I'm no dummy. I've read magazine articles about women alone, especially older women. Divorced, widowed, still single. It doesn't matter.

Depression and the myth that we no longer matter to anybody except our cats will get us down if we don't perk up and pay attention to our own needs.

Aunt Charlotte taught me that. When I left New Orleans I had no idea where I'd go, how I'd survive. All I knew was that I had to cut Louise free so she could live her own life, not mine and Josh's.

Crawling back to Tupelo with two hundred dollars in my pocket and my tail between my legs, I knocked on my parents' door and asked for a place to stay.

I'll never forget what Mama said. "If you think I'm going to put up with a squalling young 'un, you've got another think coming. This trailer's hardly big enough for Calvin and me. I raised you, now you raise yours."

I thought Daddy would intervene—he'd always been the softer one—but he didn't say a word, just shut the door in my face. That was the exact moment I figured out I didn't have a family except Louise's. Standing on Mama's rickety front steps holding onto Josh, I said, "Goodbye forever." I don't know if they were on the other side of the door listening, but I hope they were. I meant what I said, and I've never spent a day's regret over it.

After that I went to the only real home I'd ever known, Aunt Charlotte's farm.

"I'll stay just till I get on my feet," I told her.

"Piffle. Your feet belong here, and if you ever think about planting them somewhere else, I'll whip you with a cornstalk."

We stayed a year, and after I met Bill buying take-out barbecue at The Rib Cage, Aunt Charlotte said, "Good for you. Turn Tilly loose."

"Who's Tilly?" I asked.

"She was a cat owned by two old maids... And who gives a darn whether that term is politically incorrect. They never let the cat out, and then one day one of the old maids got married. On her honeymoon she wrote a note to her sister, 'Turn Tilly loose!' Good advice. Take it."

I did, and ended up with a good life. Not over-the-moon exciting as it had been with Rocky, but secure and stable with an occasional flash of real joy.

Now I want to be wise for my best friend. "Louise, I don't know much, but I do know this—we can't live in the past. Sure, I felt a little bit guilty when Harry and I did the old hubba-hubba. But I didn't let that stop me."

"I'm not fixing to do the old 'hubba-hubba.'"

"I'm not saying crawl into bed with Wayne on the first date, but still, pay your libido a little attention. Good Lord, Louise, I know you've got one. Live, girlfriend!"

"Can I just start with the Lycra sweater and red lipstick?"

"Rose, not red. And yeah, that'll do for starters,

but don't you keep me waiting too long. I'm ready for a little excitement in your e-mails."

"I gave you my cheese straw recipe."

"Goofy." I reach over and swat her arm.

"Watch out! You nearly hit that truck."

"I was six inches from his bumper."

"You were two."

"Four, and I'll not concede you another inch."

"No wonder you think Harry's so hot. You can't tell the difference between six inches and two."

"When Wayne starts after Tilly you'd best put on your glasses because I'm expecting a blow-by-blow description of every inch. By the way, Wayne who?"

"Thompson."

"Good grief. Do you reckon he's any kin to Harry?"

"It never occurred to me, but no, I doubt it. There are about two pages of Thompsons in the phone book."

"I don't know. The way our lives have intertwined you never know. Wouldn't that be a hoot? Us ending up dating cousins?"

After I drop Louise off, I go into my house,

which is empty of another living soul except King Kong. I try to pet my cat, but he acts like I've asked him to jump from a ten-story building through a hoop of fire. He leaps onto the windowsill then just sits there, grinning that self-satisfied cat grin.

"Lord, Rocky, how did I end up living with nothing but a cat?"

I do this sometimes, talk to Rocky when my life careens off and I'm not sure which way I'm heading.

If it weren't so late, I'd call Aunt Charlotte and talk to her. In spite of her eccentric notions and crazy ways, she's a wise old bird.

Instead I sit down at my piano and try to ease that aching place inside me with music. But that makes me feel even worse because I'm sitting here playing Eubie Blake's old blues song, "Gee, I Wish I Had Someone to Rock Me in the Cradle of Love."

I jump up, turn on the computer and expose my soul to Louise.

From: "Miss Sass" patsyleslie@hotmail.com
To: "The Lady" louisejernigan@yahoo.com
Sent: Wednesday, August 23, 11:30 p.m.

Subject: If life is a bowl of cherries how come I ended up with prunes?

I guess you can tell what kind of mood I'm in. Sorry if I came down so hard on you. Do what you want about sleeping with Wayne. What do I know? I'm just the girl who didn't go to college, the one whose big career achievement was singing "I'm Just a Girl Who Can't Say No" at LuLu's.

You've always been the smart one. And you've always been my friend. Whatever else happens, I don't want to lose that. Ever.

XOXO

Patsy, up too late with nobody else to talk to

I turn off the computer, take off my makeup and use my secret beauty product—a little Vaseline on top of my night cream—then lie down on my back so I won't get wrinkles on the side of my face. My other big achievement: being a woman who doesn't look or—thanks to Harry—act her age.

## CHAPTER 8

*Louise*

From: "The Lady" louisejernigan@yahoo.com
To: "Miss Sass" patsyleslie@hotmail.com
Sent: Thursday, August 24, 6:45 a.m.
Subject: Hang in there, girlfriend
Your BIG ACHIEVEMENT is being the best friend a woman ever had. And are you forgetting that you raised a son who is fine enough to make any mother strut?

I wish I didn't have to go to school. I'd come over there and we'd have tea and laugh at ourselves and cry. Yes, I said cry. I believe in that saying, "How can the soul have rainbows if it never has tears?"

Oh, Lord, look at the time. I've got to run. Come over as soon as you get off work and we can talk while I try to get used to myself in rose-colored lipstick.
XOXO
Louise, off to impart knowledge to unwilling children

I have to rush to school without waiting for her reply because I have an early-morning staff meeting. When I get home there are two e-mails waiting.

From: "Miss Sass" patsyleslie@hotmail.com
To: "The Lady" louisejernigan@yahoo.com
Sent: Thursday, August 25, 7:00 a.m.
Subject: Re: Hang in there girlfriend
If I can survive another day in the pit with Herbert, I'll take you up on that offer.
XOXO
Patsy, with feathers still falling, God knows why

From: "Miss Sass" patsyleslie@hotmail.com
To: "The Lady" louisejernigan@yahoo.com
Sent: Thursday, August 24, 3:30 p.m.
Subject: Aunt Charlotte
I took off early because Aunt Charlotte called with some big emergency, so I'm racing to the farm. Don't worry. I've got it all under control.
XOXOX
Patsy, in charge

There are two reasons I don't panic at the last e-mail: both Patsy and Aunt Charlotte define emergency as being anything more serious than a broken fingernail, and if it really were an emergency, Uncle Bradley would have phoned me.

Still, I pick up the phone and call the farm. Patsy answers.

"What's going on up there?" In the background I can hear the muted growl and hiss of Aunt Charlotte's and Uncle Bradley's voices.

"Uncle Bradley found Aunt Charlotte's John Deere keys and won't let her have them back, and she's threatening to leave."

"Oh, is that all?"

She threatens to leave at least once a month, and has ever since they married. "It keeps Bradley on his toes and keeps the excitement stirred," is what she told me once when I asked her why.

"Yeah, but this time she's got her bags packed."

"Good grief. I'll be right up there."

"You'll do no such thing. You're going to forget about everything except getting yourself all gussied up and having a good time with Wilford."

"Wayne."

"Whatever. Just have a good time. Okay?"

"I'll try."

* * *

And I really am trying, but the minute Wayne opened the door to a black Volvo—vintage, judging by the hand crank at the window—and I sat down in the front seat with my good black patent-leather purse on my knees and my tongue stuck to the roof of my mouth, I came to the conclusion that I don't know how to be fifty-five and dating.

"Is Oxford all right with you?" Wayne asks, and I don't have the foggiest idea what he's talking about.

All right for what? A topic of conversation? Dinner? Football? Sex?

Oh, help.

"I hear there's a restaurant called City Grocery that serves the best shrimp and cheese grits in Mississippi, and since I'm still fairly new here, I like to explore."

"Fine." Clinging to the handle of my purse I think about all the many things Wayne Thompson can explore in Oxford. My bold, rose-tinted lips. The front of my new, too-tight sweater. The back of my knees where I actually spritzed perfume. Not White Shoulders, which was Roy's favorite fragrance, (that would feel too much like a betrayal) but some new exotic kind that smells like tuberoses and cinnamon. I can't even remember the name.

I wonder if I'm the one in my family coming down with Alzheimer's. If Patsy were here we'd make a joke of it, this tendency of mine to be forgetful in moments of stress.

"Half-heimer's," she'd call it. "Not all the way gone, just half-assed."

All of a sudden I realize Wayne has said something to me, and I'm once again lost in my own befuddlement and anxiety.

"I like your car." That seems safe enough to say. It's a sturdy car that says, I'm my own person.

"Thank you. It's trustworthy. I think a car says a lot about its owner, don't you?"

"Well…yes…absolutely."

I twist my head toward the back seat halfway expecting Patsy to rescue me with a wisecrack the way she did when we double-dated in high school. She was always with Rocky and I was with Holder James, the only person in school nerdier than I.

But of course she's not there, and all of a sudden I see myself clearly—a past-middle-age widow who has lived her life in the safe lane, suddenly thrust into the excitement and roar of the fast lane, hanging onto her purse and hoping she doesn't get sucked under and flattened.

After Wayne drives off and I'm left standing in my front hallway with my purse dangling from my arm, I don't know whether I'm coming or going, as Aunt Charlotte would say. I'm euphoric and sad and nostalgic and scared, most of all scared.

He's stirred up feelings in me, new and exciting and yet somehow as familiar as the red Don Juan rose that climbs the gazebo in the backyard. I'm so scared by the possibilities, I don't trust myself to be alone with my thoughts.

I hang my purse on the hook in the closet, then sit in my rocking chair and pull off my pantyhose. There's a red ring around my middle where the elastic made me itch and I couldn't even scratch. Now I indulge myself in that luxury, then smear on some hydrocortisone cream before I go into my office and turn on the computer.

Patsy's e-mail is waiting.

From: "Miss Sass" patsyleslie@hotmail.com
To: "The Lady" louisejernigan@yahoo.com
Date: Thursday, August 24, 10:00 p.m.
Subject: Your DATE!!!!
Tell all! I'm dying to know!
XOXOX
Patsy

From: "The Lady" louisejernigan@yahoo.com
To: "Miss Sass" patsyleslie@hotmail.com
Date: Thursday, August 24, 11:00 p.m.
Subject: Re: Your DATE!!!!
I was scared to death at first, but Wayne's an attentive listener, and sometime between the Caesar salad and the cheese grits I began to relax. He didn't make one wrong move. I don't know what I expected—groping under the table, maybe—but he didn't even try to hold my hand. What a refreshing treat! By the time the chocolate cheesecake came, I had almost quit feeling guilty and was actually enjoying myself.

By the way, what happened at Aunt Charlotte's?
Hugs,
Louise


From: "Miss Sass" patsyleslie@hotmail.com
To: "The Lady" louisejernigan@yahoo.com
Date: Thursday, August 24, 11:05 p.m.
Subject: Re: Your Date!!!!
Can't you guess? Uncle Bradley said, "Darlin',
there's no need for you to leave the farm. I'll go
myself." Naturally he just went out back to his
workshop and stayed about fifteen minutes, then
came back with one of those big boxes of chocolates he keeps stashed out there. When I left she
was hand-feeding him the ones with nuts in the
center and he was calling her "love" and "baby"
and "my little girl," and she was grinning like the
Cheshire cat. I don't know why she's never caught
on about the chocolates. She's nobody's dummy.
What do you mean…"feeling guilty?" If you say
"about betraying Roy," I'm going to personally
march over there and turn King Kong loose in
your prize petunias. He was a good man, but by
George he was no plaster saint. If you'll care to
remember, he was the one who didn't want you

to go back to school to get your Ph.D. Quit deifying him!

And if you say "because we're a certain age and ought to be satisfied with good health and a grand-baby and Social Security on the way" I'm going to barf right here on my white Hollywood rug.

XOXO

Patsy, getting pissed at you


From: "The Lady" louisejernigan@yahoo.com
To: "Miss Sass" patsyleslie@hotmail.com
Date: Thursday, August 24, 11:08 p.m.
Subject: Re: Your Date!!!!

What Hollywood rug? White??????

XOXO

L

P.S. Aunt Charlotte knows about the chocolate stash. She just pretends she doesn't. It's all part of her game to keep the mystery and excitement in her marriage. What about the John Deere keys?


From: "Miss Sass" patsyleslie@hotmail.com
To: "The Lady" louisejernigan@yahoo.com
Date: Thursday, August 24, 11:10 p.m.
Subject: Re: Your Date!!!!

White and shaggy and lush. Just right for seduc-
tion. I stopped at the mall on the way back from
Aunt Charlotte's tonight. Can't you just picture
Harry and me rolling around on that rug?
Don't sidetrack me. What about your famous
guilt trip?
XOXOX
Patsy
P.S. Uncle Bradley still has the keys, but I predict
not for long.


From: "The Lady" louisejernigan@yahoo.com
To: "Miss Sass" patsyleslie@hotmail.com
Date: Thursday, August 24, 11:12 p.m.
Subject: Re: Your Date!!!!
You hit the nail on the head re: my guilt trip. I
know, I *know*. Nobody was ever as good in real
life as we make them out to be when they're
dead. Still, Roy set the bar high and I keep
watching to see how Wayne is going to measure
up. *Sigh!*
Listen, I've got to hit the hay. Tomorrow's a school
day. Can you get me an appointment with your
hairstylist for Saturday?
L

From: "Miss Sass" patsyleslie@hotmail.com
To: "The Lady" louisejernigan@yahoo.com
Date: Thursday, August 24, 11:15 p.m.
Subject: Re: Your Date!!!!
Wait a minute, you can't go to bed yet! Did Wayne kiss you?
And you bet your britches I'll take you to get a new hairdo. I'm thinking short and sassy. Boy, won't the kids be surprised! I'll even take you to Pier One and we'll get you a white rug. Always be ready, that's my motto!
XOXOX
Patsy


From: "The Lady" louisejernigan@yahoo.com
To: "Miss Sass" patsyleslie@hotmail.com
Date: Thursday, August 24, 11:17 p.m.
Subject: Re: Your Date!!!!
Yes, he kissed me, and it was nice. Not the modern movie kind of nice. More like Rock Hudson and Doris Day in those fifties comedies way back before everybody found out he didn't even like women.
Love and good night, (I mean it, Patsy, I've got to go to bed!)
Louise

I go to bed, but now, of course, I can't go to sleep because I'm thinking about the kiss and how I wasn't sure whether I should or whether I even wanted to and how I just stood there hanging on to my front doorknob like an idiot until Wayne bent down and removed the indecision and the mystery. It couldn't have lasted more than a few seconds but while it was happening, it seemed like a lifetime.

You've heard of drowning people whose whole lives flash before their eyes? That's exactly the way I felt when Wayne cupped my face and pressed his lips against mine. I had to stand on tiptoe and hang on to the front of his shirt to keep from being off balance. While all these sensations ripped through me—shock, pleasure, hope—I kept seeing Roy buying our first boat and bending over Diana's crib and brushing his teeth and tracking mud into the kitchen and pulling off my bra in the middle of the day right under the skylight that allows for no invention.

Jerked upright by memory, I switch on the bedside lamp and stare at the picture of Roy and me aboard the *Louise*. Just stare. When my lips start trembling, I press my hands over my mouth.

Once you've known great love, is it possible to love again? And if you do, what happens to all the pictures from your former life? Do you hide them in a drawer so nobody gets his feelings hurt or do you leave them out so they can waylay you with memories?

I know all this sounds silly and insignificant, but it's these small details stitched together that create the fabric of our lives. Getting up in the middle of the night for a bite of peanut butter on a teaspoon dipped straight into the jar. Arguing over who squeezed the toothpaste in the middle and who left the cap off the shampoo. Deciding whether to go out for pizza or just order in because it's raining and besides you don't want to miss *Wheel of Fortune* because last night one of the contestants won a car and you weren't there to see it.

I rub my hand over the face in the picture frame. Roy, what in the world am I going to do? I switch off the light and lie there in the dark, waiting, but there's no answer, no great cosmic wisdom whispered in my ear because I'm listening with my heart and soul. Just the *tick-tock* of the hall clock, the drip from a leaky faucet in the bathroom I forgot to mention so Josh can fix it, and the thump of my own heart reminding me that I'm alive.

*Yes*, I think. Just that. *Yes*.

## CHAPTER 9

*Patsy*

**Anybody** watching my red Jag fly down Robins, hang a right on Gloster and head toward Saltillo would say, There go the future grandmas for another Sunday dinner with their children.

They'd be right about only one thing—the dinner.

Nobody in his right mind would describe the two of us as grandmas. Louise is wearing blue jeans she had to lie down on the bed and wedge herself into before she could zip. I know because I was the one who told her to do it. And I'm showing so much leg under my new red Lycra skirt you'd think I was fixing to try out for the Folies Bergère. Plus, our hair looks like it was styled with a Mixmaster—Louise's, thanks to her new cut and plenty of gel and mine, compliments of Harry.

I was just getting all gussied up for church this morning when he called and asked if he could come over. "I can't stand to be without you another minute, Patsy," is what he told me, and naturally, when it comes to a choice between a Sunday sermon and a Sunday-morning quickie, I'll go for the quickie every time.

And I know Harry said love is better if you keep it to yourself, but I'm feeling so self-satisfied, I can't help but brag to Louise. Besides, she's the Sphinx when it comes to secrets, and I figure she might need a little inspiration now that she's dating Wayne.

"Harry's got the cutest little café au lait birthmark on his left butt cheek. And he's really, really hot. I'm talking almost as good a Rocky. Lord, this morning he tied me to the bedpost."

"You let him tie you up? That could be dangerous, Patsy."

"Jeez, Louise. Haven't you ever heard of bondage?"

"Well, of course I have, but I don't think women our age are supposed to actually engage in it."

"Age doesn't have a thing to do with it. Besides, Louise, if you never want anything but the missionary position, Wayne's not going to know if you're having a good time or praying."

"Hush, Patsy. And for your information, I'm not doing anything with Wayne."

"Not yet, you mean."

I wheel the Jag into the curving driveway in front of Josh and Diana's sprawling ranch-style house, and out comes my son, looking so much like Rocky it takes me a minute to get my breath back. When he sees my hair, he does a double take.

"Brace yourself," I tell Louise, and then I tug down my skirt and step out of the car.

"Good God, Mama, what did you do with your hair? And where's the rest of your skirt?"

Glancing from me to Louise, he gets this confused look on his face that makes me want to pat him on the head the way I did when he was three and left his favorite toy outside to be ruined by the rain.

"Diana?" He strides toward the front door,

sticks his head in and calls, "Honey? Can you come here a minute?"

We don't faze Diana. "Oh, my gosh. You two look fabulous." But we don't fool her, either. "What in the world's going on?"

This is the part I've been dreading. I'm not usually one to pussyfoot around, but I guess my own mama spoiled me on the subject of boyfriends. I never could please her about the men in my life. Or anything else, for that matter.

"You know about Louise's boyfriend?"

"He's just a friend," Louise says, but when I give her a "help me out, here" look, she reaches over to squeeze my hand.

"Well, I've got one, too."

"When do we get to meet him?" This is typical Josh. Grabbing his sword, jumping on his white stallion and charging to the rescue before anybody has even declared a war.

"Not till I say so, and that's all I'm going to say on the subject. Let's go eat dinner and talk about baby names. I'm still voting for Patsy Louise."

"So am I."

I can always count on Louise. And, boy, when we join forces, not even Napoleon's battalions could move us.

Still, on the way home I have to admit that Josh has a point about meeting Harry.

"Does this mean you're getting serious about him?" Louise asks.

"I'm not picking out rings or anything, but still we fit together like Rogers and Astaire."

"Don't you think it's too early to tell? You and I fit like Lucy and Ethel, but that doesn't mean I want to marry you."

"Look, Louise, he's not Rocky and never will be, but he makes me feel happy to be alive. At the very least it's time for you to meet him."

I don't believe in introspection. In my opinion all it's good for is to give you a headache. I don't want to be a better me; I just want to be *me*.

Still, when I get home I can't help but reflect on my future.

From: "Miss Sass" patsyleslie@hotmail.com
To: "The Lady" louisejernigan@yahoo.com

Date: Sunday, August 27, 7:00 p.m.

Subject: A Harryless Life

When I think about doing nothing for the rest of my life except going to bridge on Tuesdays and quilting every other Thursdays and listening to Mary Jo's endless palavering about who's lost ten pounds and what kind of diet they're on and whether they've had a face-lift, I want to hide under my bed and never come out. I know I could be doing something lofty like improving my mind by reading John Grisham (bet you thought I'd say Shakespeare, didn't you?), but you know me. I'm too lazy and unmotivated for that. On the other hand, Harry takes no effort whatsoever. He just makes me feel good. And is that so bad? I'm not the kind of person to go around pondering the meaning of life. I just want to enjoy it. And I'm not so sure I was doing much of that before Harry came along.

XOXOX

Patsy, just wondering


From: "The Lady" louisejernigan@yahoo.com

To: "Miss Sass" patsyleslie@hotmail.com

Date: Sunday, August 27, 7:30 p.m.

Subject: Re: A Harryless Life

I'm coming right over. With my pajamas and toothbrush. Do you have any popcorn?
XOXOX
Louise

From: "Miss Sass" patsyleslie@hotmail.com
To: "The Lady" louisejernigan@yahoo.com
Date: Sunday, August 27, 7:32 p.m.
Subject: Re: My Harryless Life
No, but I've got the butter. Bring a bag.
XOXO
Patsy, grateful

*Louise*

Patsy meets me at the door in black fuzzy house shoes with cat faces while King Kong switches his tail and glares at me from his red silk pillow on the sofa.

"Your cat hates me."

"He hates everybody. He only tolerates me because I'm the source of his Meow Mix."

Suddenly Patsy's shoulders slump, and instead of looking six feet tall and capable of leaping small buildings at a single bound, the way she always has to me, she shrinks to an ordinary woman with too many wrinkles to wear pancake makeup and too many heartaches to fool her best friend with a brave smile.

"If you could have one day back in your life, what would it be, Louise? Just one day?"

"I think it would be the day we brought Diana home from the hospital and Roy stood over her crib for an hour watching her breathe. 'Did you ever think we'd be part of a miracle?' he asked, and I'll never forget that he had tears in his eyes."

"Mine would be the day before Rocky died when he talked about driving to the farm to visit Aunt Charlotte and Uncle Bradley, and I said, 'Honey, I think it's going to rain tomorrow. Why don't we wait till next weekend?' And so he went to Piggly Wiggly to get hot dogs instead of driving to Birmingham Ridge, and a lightning bolt snuffed him out while I was at home putting charcoal on the grill."

"It wasn't your fault, Patsy."

"I know, but sometime I wonder if he'd still be alive if I hadn't said 'wait.'"

We go into the kitchen and I start popping the corn while Patsy sits at the table with her absurdly large house shoes propped on another chair.

"Would you think I'm being foolish if I decided to marry Harry knowing I'll never love him the way I did Rocky?"

"You'll never love anybody the way you loved Rocky."

"Yeah, but what would you think about me marrying him? I don't know that much about him except how he makes me feel. Josh is going to want to get his pedigree and maybe call in the FBI for a background check, and Diana's going to worry that I haven't known him long enough. I'm probably just a foolish, lonely old woman."

"I'm the old one. Remember? You always tell everybody you're forty and call yourself middle-aged."

"Seriously, Louise."

I pour the steaming popcorn into a big copper-bottomed bowl, add melted butter and set it on the table between us.

"Sometimes the wisest person you know is that little voice whispering in your ear. Call it instinct, call it angels. It doesn't matter. All I know is that it tells you the bone-deep truth."

"The truth is I could be dead next year." Patsy grabs a handful of corn. "Or I could be in Hawaii with Harry surfing."

"You're afraid of water."

"Well, don't you think it's high time I learned how to swim? After all, I'm a forty-year-old woman."

I toss a kernel of corn at her, and King Kong comes into the kitchen and rubs his arched back against her shoe, and Patsy's smile is back, this time with the heartache pushed so far back you hardly even notice.

I haven't seen Patsy this anxious since I spent the night with her nearly two weeks ago and we ate too much popcorn and stayed up too late.

I'm supposed to meet Harry tonight, and I brought over Don Juan roses for the occasion. She has moved them six times.

"Do you think they look all right in the

middle of the table or do they look better on the piano?" she asked.

"Leave them on the table. They look great. Everything's going to be fine."

"I don't know. I've never cooked for Harry. What if the roast beef's not done in the middle?"

"Then we'll eat around the edges. Relax, Patsy. He's just a man."

"No, he's Harry. My Lord, Louise, I've been looking at rings."

"Harry's asked you to marry him?"

"Not exactly."

"Maybe you ought to swim around in the shallows before you jump in the deep end, Patsy."

"You know me. Caution has never been my strong suit. Actually he doesn't know I'm looking, but I have a feeling he's going to ask me soon. He was absolutely thrilled about meeting you tonight. And he wants to meet the children."

The phone cuts Patsy short and she takes it in the den.

A few minutes later she comes back in, plops on a kitchen chair and says, "It was just Mary Jo. Wondering if I was ever coming back to bridge and quilting. I started to say, Screw bridge and quilting."

"Well, what did you tell her?"

"Screw bridge. I left quilting up in the air."

The phone calls Patsy to the den once more, and while she's gone I rearrange the roses for lack of something to do. Harry's late. Another mark against him, in my book.

"Harry's not coming." Patsy announces this in a flat voice, standing in the kitchen doorway with her arms wrapped around herself. "He's sick."

"Oh."

"Well, he is."

"I didn't say he wasn't."

"It was the way you said it, Louise."

"I'm sorry, Patsy. I'm sure he would have come if he could. But there'll be other times." I want to find this Harry goober and snatch him bald-headed. Unless he was vomiting up blood, he should have been here. "Listen, I'll cook and the two of you can come over to my house. Maybe we can make it a foursome. You can meet Wayne and I can meet Harry at the same time."

"Sure. That will be great." Patsy's getting her bounce back. "Shoot, that just means we get to eat the whole pie."

"What kind?"

"Key lime. Compliments of me and Betty Crocker."

When I leave, I realize I've never seen Patsy this uncertain, and I don't like it. Already I'm building up a case against this Harry character, preparing not to like him. After all, a woman thinking of marriage should be glowing with confidence, certain that the heart she has offered is being treated with tender loving care.

Take Wayne and me, for instance. Even though we've only been dating a few weeks, there's nothing I can't tell him, no situation where I can imagine being as unsure of myself as Patsy is tonight.

Well, sex maybe, but thank God Wayne's courting me slowly and waiting till I'm ready. On the other hand, this Harry twerp rushed Patsy into bed, got her so hot and bothered she can't think straight anymore.

## CHAPTER 10

*Louise*

**When** I look back on it, I'd have to say that Harry was the one responsible for me having sex with Wayne. We were having dessert at Woody's while I told him about Harry standing up Patsy.

"And if he'd been so sick," I said, "why didn't he call her before she did all that cooking? It all sounded fishy to me, and I'm afraid Patsy's going to get hurt."

"You're a wonderful woman, Louise, to be so concerned for your friend."

"Why…thank you."

"I don't think I've ever known a woman quite like you."

He was so kind and understanding that when he invited me to his apartment for after-dinner coffee, I said yes. Later, when he kissed me, one thing led to another, and before you know it I was in Wayne's bedroom spread across his green comforter like a ripe peach, feeling stirrings I haven't felt since Roy died.

If we had been in the bed I'd shared with my husband, I couldn't have done it. If the lights had been on I couldn't have bared my body. If Wayne hadn't been so understanding about Patsy, I might not have given in. So many ifs.

Another big one…if I had expected the earth to move, I wouldn't have had sex with Wayne that Thursday night. But I had no expectations, just a need that was making itself known in a way too urgent to ignore.

Wayne was efficient and capable and I guess I was on autopilot, because when it was all over, the only thing I could remember was that he wasn't shaped like Roy who seemed built to touch me in the places that mattered most.

When Wayne left me at my front door, I went straight to the closet and took Roy's raincoat off the hanger, then stood there with it pressed to my cheek for a very long time. Finally I folded it, then put it in the cedar chest with his good wool sweaters and his winter gloves—things I'm going to give to the Salvation Army when I get up enough nerve.

Feeling a sense of satisfaction and accomplishment I haven't felt in a long time, I went to the computer to tell Patsy. Lord, that's me dead out. Always the achiever. So here is one more thing I achieved: being a widow who finally understands that you have many needs and it's no crime if you take care of the physical ones, even if you're not madly in love.

From: "The Lady" louisejernigan@yahoo.com
To: "Miss Sass" patsyleslie@hotmail.com
Date: Thursday, September 14, 10:30 p.m.
Subject: My new love life
Well, I finally did it! It's sort of like riding a bicycle: you never forget.
XOXO
Louise

From: "Miss Sass" patsyleslie@hotmail.com
To: "The Lady" louisejernigan@yahoo.com

Date: Thursday, September 14, 10:35 p.m.
Subject: Re: My new love life
Congratulations! But, girl, if you think sex is a
bicycle you need more help than I can give you.
XOXO
Patsy, who says "welcome to the club."

It turns out I didn't need help. Wayne and I are establishing a routine as comfortable as my old one, except exponentially more exciting—dinner on Thursdays in little out-of-the-ways places he loves followed by coffee and sex, so far only at his place, but I think I would be okay now with mine. I really do.

Now I'm on the way home from bridge (sans Patsy) wishing it was Thursday instead of Tuesday and I had Wayne to look forward to. Mary Jo keeps prying about why Patsy gave up bridge, and if Aunt Charlotte has called one time she's called ten. The prodigal son, Jerry, is coming for a visit.

"You've got to help me cook up some casseroles that are fit to eat," she's saying now as I try to navigate the traffic on Gloster Street and hold on to the cell phone at the same time.

# The Harlequin Reader Service® — Here's how it works:

If offer card is missing write to: Harlequin Reader Service, 3010 Walden Ave., P.O. Box 1867, Buffalo NY 14240-1867

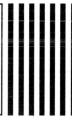

NO POSTAGE
NECESSARY
IF MAILED
IN THE
UNITED STATES

## BUSINESS REPLY MAIL

FIRST-CLASS MAIL   PERMIT NO. 717-003   BUFFALO, NY

POSTAGE WILL BE PAID BY ADDRESSEE

HARLEQUIN READER SERVICE
3010 WALDEN AVE
PO BOX 1867
BUFFALO NY 14240-9952

# GET FREE BOOKS and FREE GIFTS WHEN YOU PLAY THE...

## Lucky 7

### SLOT MACHINE GAME!

*Just scratch off the silver box with a coin. Then check below to see the gifts you get!*

# YES! I have scratched off the silver box. Please send me the 2 free Harlequin Romance® books and 2 free gifts for which I qualify. I understand I am under no obligation to purchase any books, as explained on the back of this card.

**386 HDL EF4U**                    **186 HDL EF4N**

| | |
|---|---|
| FIRST NAME | LAST NAME |

ADDRESS

| | |
|---|---|
| APT.# | CITY |

| | |
|---|---|
| STATE/PROV. | ZIP/POSTAL CODE |

| 7 | 7 | 7 | **Worth TWO FREE BOOKS plus 2 BONUS Mystery Gifts!** |
|---|---|---|---|
| 🍒 | 🍒 | 🍒 | **Worth TWO FREE BOOKS!** |
| ♣ | ♣ | ♣ | **Worth ONE FREE BOOK!** |
| 🔔 | 🔔 | 🍒 | **TRY AGAIN!** |

www.eHarlequin.com

(H-R-12/06)

DETACH AND MAIL CARD TODAY! © 2000 HARLEQUIN ENTERPRISES LTD. ® and TM are trademarks owned and used by the trademark owner and/or its licensee.

"I will, Aunt Charlotte."

"When? He's coming tomorrow and if you don't cook something decent he'll act like he's starving to death." She's a minute person, wants everything done immediately.

"Tomorrow, after school."

I had meant to get a touch-up on this golden-brown hair color that I'm finally getting used to, but that will have to wait. At least while Jerry's visiting, Aunt Charlotte won't be carrying on a running battle with Uncle Bradley over the John Deere keys.

Inside I toss my purse onto the closet hook and climb into pajamas and bed. Tomorrow I'll need all the energy I can get to deal with all the cooking and a cousin without a single redeeming quality if you don't count that he sends Christmas cards on time.

The phone jars me awake and as I pick up the receiver I squint at the glowing face of the bedside clock. 11:30. Diana?

"What? What?" I shout into the receiver, expecting the worst.

"Sorry, baby, did I wake you?" It's Wayne. "I was

in the mood for a little fun and games and wondered if I could come over."

Suddenly I'm not merely a woman who does errands for Aunt Charlotte and cooks Sunday dinner for the kids and plays bridge on Tuesday nights. I'm a woman who drives men mad with desire in the middle of the night.

"Yes," I say, and he's knocking on my back door before I have time to brush my teeth and put on lipstick. Thank God I went to bed in mascara.

I tease him about coming in the back and he says, "I thought it would add to the excitement."

I guess it does because when I reach for the light switch and he says, "Leave it on," I do, not caring a whit that the skin around my belly looks like it needs pressing and my breasts look like they need a good forklift.

All of a sudden Wayne's tying my arms to the bedpost with red silk scarves. After the fact, he says, "Do you mind?" but by now I don't have a mind, only a body filled with lust.

Who would have dreamed a woman my age

who looks like an eggplant naked could have erotic feelings a twenty-year-old would envy?

The next morning I have to drink two good strong cups of coffee before I can get myself awake. In the light of day I see last night for what it was—a rash action that leaves more questions than answers. I hurry to the computer to have some serious girl talk with Patsy. Her e-mail is waiting.

From: "Miss Sass" patsyleslie@hotmail.com
To: "The Lady" louisejernigan@yahoo.com
Date: Wednesday, October 11, 6:45 a.m.
Subject: HARRY!!!!
We're not talking diamonds and vows yet, but boy is that man hot for me. We had another over-the-moon session with red scarves last night. I'm willing to bet he pops the question next Tuesday night.
XOXOX
Patsy, glowing but not from any blush

I stare at this message dumbfounded while last night flashes before my eyes—lights on for the first time, me thrashing around in red scarves,

Wayne vanishing under the covers with his left butt cheek sporting a little café au lait birthmark.

Worst of all, it was almost midnight, plenty of time for him to have his way with Patsy then sneak through the hedge with his red scarves and his lusty libido and all his big talk about fun and games. Just what kind of game is he playing?

I feel so hot I have to strip off my sweater. Neon-green Lycra, for Pete's sake. I look like somebody doing a bad imitation of a watermelon.

Underneath I'm wearing a wispy bra that would barely hold a sneeze, let alone my two Saturn Five missiles. What on earth was I thinking, fixing to parade around at school advertising the goods? My lord, I look like a woman who has gone goofy over sex.

But in my own defense, I'll have to say, I suppose I wouldn't be the first.

Racing to my closet, I jerk on a nice white cotton blouse with a Peter Pan collar, and then sit down to answer Patsy's e-mail. She'll get suspicious if I don't.

From: "The Lady" louisejernigan@yahoo.com
To: "Miss Sass" patsyleslie@hotmail.com
Date: Wednesday, October 11, 6:55 a.m.
Subject: Re: HARRY!!!
Are you in love with him, Patsy?
XOXO
Louise, in a hurry

While I wait for her answer I flip through the Thompsons in the phone book. Adam, Albert, Charles, Chuck, David, Darrell, Dwayne. Skipping to the Hs I find H. W., Harry, Harvey, Herbert. The Ws yield W. A., W. D., W. P., Waymon, Wexford, Wilfred, but no Wayne. Panicked I look again, but then remember that the phone book is only three months old and I don't know when Wayne moved to Tupelo. Maybe he didn't have time to get his name in. Or he could be W. A., W. D. or W. P.

From: "Miss Sass" patsyleslie@hotmail.com
To: "The Lady" louisejernigan@yahoo.com
Date: Wednesday, October 11, 7:00 p.m.
Subject: Re: HARRY!!!
I don't know. He's not Rocky, but life's more fun with

him than it was without him, and shouldn't that count for something? Jeez, Louise, we're no spring chickens! It's not like there's going to be another Rocky Delgado waiting behind every gardenia bush.
XOXOX
Patsy, off to work, SMILING

Or he could be H. W., Harry Wayne. I fret all day, and by the time I head home from school all I want is to put my feet up and forget about Harry being Wayne and Wayne being Harry who has a penchant for red scarves and too many women.

Of course, I'm being ridiculous. I'll just ask him. That's all. I won't get the chance today, though, because Aunt Charlotte's red Dodge Ram pickup truck is in my driveway and she's sitting on the front porch in a white wicker rocking chair.

Did she get confused and forget that I was coming to her house to cook for Jerry?

"Hello, Aunt Charlotte." When I kiss her cheek I surreptitiously check to see if there's any blankness or confusion in her eyes. "Where's Uncle Bradley?"

"I've left the old fart. I'm moving in with you."

"What happened?" I sink into the wicker chaise next to her. If I had a pillow under my head and an afghan for my feet I'd fall asleep out of pure stress.

"Bradley and Jerry are in cahoots about my tractor. And all because of a little mishap."

I'm almost afraid to ask. "What little mishap?"

"It got stuck in forward gear, and the only way I could stop it was run into something solid."

An embankment, is what I'm thinking. The farm is full of them. Of maybe some nice, flexible bales of hay.

"What did you hit, Aunt Charlotte?"

"Bradley's shed. He needn't have acted so huffy. All I did was take out the west side. Of course, after we finally got the John Deere unstuck and backed out, the roof caved in."

"Good Lord."

"You don't have to look so stricken. He'll come a' running when he misses my cooking."

"You can't cook, Aunt Charlotte."

"That's the beauty of it. I'm so bad that when

I do fix something decent Bradley's so grateful he acts like he's married to Julia Child."

She pulls down her glasses and peers at me over the top, and I'd swear her eyes are twinkling as if she's pulled off the best stunt since Houdini's underwater escape.

"Have you got any chocolate cherry cake, Louise? It takes lots of carbohydrates to carry on like a sixteen-year-old."

She's not telling me anything I don't know. Carrying on till all hours of the night, then worrying all day about the identity of the man I'm dating is enough to make a woman eat a pound of butter straight from the carton.

"I don't have a cake but I'll make one. Give me your keys and I'll get your bag first."

"What's that on your neck?"

"What's what?"

"It looks like a hickey to me. Have you been bolly foxing around?"

"I don't 'bolly fox,' Aunt Charlotte," I say as I put her bag inside and go into the kitchen.

"I'm not judging. It's high time, that's what I

say. Just be careful that he's not the bossy kind, like Bradley."

"That's not what I'm worried about, Aunt Charlotte."

And then because she's the only mother I've ever really known and because I know she'll listen without passing judgment, I tell her about Harry/Wayne while I mix a box of cherry pie filling with a big batch of chocolate cake mix.

The scent of cocoa mingled with cherries rises from the bowl. I feel better already.

"And here's another thing, Aunt Charlotte." I turn off the mixer, then hand her one beater to lick while I lick the other. "Harry dates Patsy on only Tuesdays and Wayne has never been with me except on Thursday. Until late last night. Which was Tuesday."

"How late?"

"Midnight."

"Whooee! This is almost as good as wrecking Bradley's workshop with my tractor." She peers around my shoulder while I pour batter into two round pans. "Can I lick the bowl?"

"Of course, I could be making mountains out of molehills." I hand her the bowl and my big wooden stirring spoon. "What am I going to do?"

"Sneak around and find out stuff."

"I don't sneak."

"Well, I do."

I think she's kidding, but I'm scared to ask.

"I'm sure this will all clear itself up. Patsy calls me a worrywart. I'll just talk to Wayne. He'll probably laugh his head off."

"Which one?"

Letting this remark pass, I pick up the phone and dial Wayne's cell phone.

"No time like the present." I say this with a lot of false bravado. Actually I feel like an air mattress that somebody's poked a hole in and then stomped on a couple of times.

"Hey there, Wayne! How are you!" Lord, I'm talking in exclamation points. I ought to take up acting.

"Great. Especially after last night. I can't wait for tomorrow night."

"That's why I'm calling. My Aunt Charlotte is

visiting and I thought I'd just make dinner here so you two can meet."

There's a pause big enough to run a rig through. This makes me nervous. And suspicious.

"Actually, since I'll be cooking anyway, I was thinking about inviting Patsy. And Harry."

When God passed out good looks I was hiding under a barrel, but nobody can ever say I wasn't on the front row when he handed out brains.

Finally Wayne says, "That sounds like fun," and I blow like a filly trying to qualify for the Kentucky Derby. I even smile and wink at Aunt Charlotte while I chat with him about roast beef versus chicken and dumplings.

"What did he say?" Aunt Charlotte asks the minute I hang up.

"He's coming. Everything's all right. I'm going to call Patsy. Shoot I might as well call Diana and Josh, too. And why don't you call Uncle Bradley and Jerry. We'll make it a big family get-together."

"Piffle, I don't want Bradley thinking I'm easy. Let him rattle around that big old house for a while by himself and see how he likes it. He'll think twice the next time he tries to tell me what to do."

I get up at five so I can make the pecan pies before I go to school. Some women would say, Why slave in the kitchen? Order takeout. But the kitchen is my haven. Like my grandmother, I have made it a place that symbolizes all that's good about a family: the cookie jar that sucks in children bursting to talk about their school day; the freshly brewed gourmet coffee that lures husband and friends to the table where they'll sit with knees touching while they solve problems and plan futures; the morning sun slashing through the east window and making a warm spot on the tile just right for standing in bare feet and simply being.

Standing in the path of sunlight and memories, I'm fluting the edges of the pie crust when I notice a movement in the hedges between my house and Patsy's. King Kong? If that mean cat escapes again, Patsy will have a fit.

I shove the pies in the oven, wipe my hands on

a dish towel, then barrel out the back door and through the hedges. There's someone on Patsy's porch. Should I call the police? Call Patsy? Scream?

The intruder moves again and I see blue jeans and a hot-pink T-shirt, the big green John Deere logo on the front.

Aunt Charlotte. Doing Lord only knows what. I sprint that way, grateful for small favors.

At least she's wearing clothes.

"Aunt Charlotte, what are you doing on Patsy's front porch?"

"Checking her mail. What else?"

She has a handful of Patsy's mail and is riffling through it like the Gestapo.

"Put that back. Good grief, Aunt Charlotte. It's a federal offense to be caught tampering with the U.S. Mail."

"It ought to be a federal offense to go catting through the hedges from one house to another, but I didn't hear you blessing out that Harry/Wayne scuzz bucket."

"I'm not blessing you out. We've got to get out of here."

I take Patsy's mail and put it back, then try to lead Aunt Charlotte off the porch, which proves to be like trying to lead a herd of turkeys to the Thanksgiving chopping block.

"Wait," she says. "There was a card in there that looked interesting. Maybe it was from him. I think it said Thompson."

"Come on, Aunt Charlotte."

"We could steam it open, then put it back."

"No."

"She'd never know."

"I would. I'm not about to stoop to this sort of skullduggery with my best friend."

"Had you rather just go on sharing a boy-friend with her?"

Inside I see Patsy's bedroom light switch on. What will I say if she catches us here? Hi, Patsy, we were just snooping.

We hightail it, and when we get back to my kitchen I'm so mad it takes a while before I notice the red light on my message machine.

"Hi, this is Wayne. I had to come into work early and just got zapped with a project that's going to take till midnight to finish. Sorry about the dinner, babe. Can I take a rain check?"

"See?" With her hands on her hips and her white hair sticking up in sleep-tossed tufts, Aunt Charlotte looks like a small, vengeful, molting bird. "I told you. That scoundrel's fixing to break both your hearts."

"He just canceled dinner, that's all. Besides, Harry will be here tonight with Patsy, and we can get everything cleared up."

"Piffle, do you think I was born yesterday?"

"No, you were born in—"

"Don't say it or I'll cut you out of my will. But then, of course, I'd have to leave everything to that shiftless Jerry."

The oven timer rings, and I take the pies out. It's time to get dressed for school. Horrible thought. Aunt Charlotte with the run of the neighborhood.

"Aunt Charlotte, can I trust you to be good while I'm at school?"

"You can't trust me as far as you can throw me."

"I'm serious. Will you promise to quit snooping around Patsy's house?"

"Okay. I won't snoop. But that's all I'm promising."

On the way to school I phone Diana to let her know that Wayne won't be coming to dinner.

"I'm disappointed, Mom. Josh and I wanted to meet him."

"I'm not serious about him, Diana."

"Maybe not, but he's been good for you, brought you out of your shell."

I picture myself as a slow-moving box turtle, carrying my protective shell everywhere I go in case I need to duck inside and hide. *Okay.* Maybe I didn't get a Ph.D. and set the educational world on its ear, but at least I've crawled out from my shell and discovered there's more to life than playing it safe.

*Patsy*

From: "Miss Sass" patsyleslie@hotmail.com
To: "The Lady" louisejernigan@yahoo.com
Date: Thursday, October 12, 7:00 a.m.
Subject: Burglars

I thought I heard burglars on my front porch this morning. Did you hear anything? This used to be a safe neighborhood, but ever since somebody broke into Clyde's backyard down the street and stole his Venus statue right out of the middle of his prize daylilies, I've been wondering if I ought to get a watchdog. Of course, King Kong would have a fit, but why should I let a cat run my life? By the way, I've been thinking that after I marry Harry, I'll quit my job at the bank. Heck, we might even build a house out in the country close to Aunt Charlotte. He's always talking about how nice it would be to live in the country where you can see the moon and stars instead of pale versions of them blotted out by city lights.

It would be awful to leave you here, though. Maybe you can come, too. Maybe Aunt Charlotte would sell us a couple of acres and we could both build close to her.

I can hardly wait for tonight. I hope Harry and Wayne get along the way Roy and Bill did. It will be fun going into our golden years, a foursome.

Gotta run.

XOXO

Patsy, wearing a Lycra skirt and three-inch heels just to piss Herbert off

While I put on makeup, I race between the bathroom and my desk so I can check for Louise's response, but I guess she's got her hands full with Aunt Charlotte. That year I lived with her, she kept me so busy with schemes to get Uncle Bradley's goat that I didn't have time to worry about being a single parent or the rift I'd caused between Louise and me. I didn't have time to mourn the loss of Rocky and the loss of my big career dreams.

Oh, I know working at LuLu's was not a career, but it was a foot in the door, a chance to sing to a crowd, half of them too drunk to tell whether I sounded like Edith Piaf or a wailing cat in a tin bucket and the other half too busy trying to put the make on the cocktail waitresses to even listen.

Still, I was doing what I loved and heading somewhere, moving up, moving on, testing my wings. Most of all, I was with someone who loved me. Now I feel like somebody has taken the pinking shears and clipped my flying feathers. The only time I feel like I'm flying nowadays is when I'm in bed with Harry.

I know I'm a shallow woman, but it's not all about sex, either. Harry fuels my dream of family, of coming home every night to a real home filled with love. Is that too much to ask?

At the bank I wonder how many more times I'll have to park my flashy red car in their tacky lot, which does nothing to show it off. I wonder how many more times I'll have to walk through those hateful double glass doors and endure Herbert's pursed-lipped look. I flounce past her, daring her to comment on my attire. I'll quit this job in a New York minute. I can, now that I have Harry.

The thought of showing him off tonight makes the day go faster. By the time I get home I'm so excited I barely get my key in the door. I'll wear my new yellow jumpsuit with just enough Lycra to show everybody that women of a certain age with generous hips don't have to worry that they don't look like young supermodels. Just smile and flaunt it. That's all.

I head next door to help with last-minute food preparation. I had hoped to be the first one there so I could have a private chat with Louise about moving to the farm and building little side-by-side houses, but Josh's car is in the driveway and who should let me in but Aunt Charlotte?

Without fanfare she says, "I want you to march in there and tell Louise I wasn't hurting a thing deadheading those roses."

Running to keep up with her, I toss my purse in the direction of the sofa and hope it hits. When we get to the kitchen, Louise says, "I heard that, Aunt Charlotte."

"Piffle. Who cares?"

"You deadhead roses all the time, Louise," I say. "What was wrong with Aunt Charlotte doing it?"

Josh looks up from the salads he and Diana are fixing. "I'd be careful if I were you, Mama." He winks and Diana grins and I have this feeling that I've stepped off in a pile of dog doo. Again.

"They weren't my roses." Louise turns off the heat under the almonds she's browning for green beans almandine (I hope), and turns it up under the unrepentant little Julius Caesar sitting in the kitchen chair with her fighting boots on. "They belonged to Irma June Lipincott."

"Well, her roses needed it." Aunt Charlotte pinches some crust off the pecan pie and pokes it in her mouth. "I was doing her a favor. She ought to have been kissing my feet instead of acting like a jackass."

Louise set the pies out of Aunt Charlotte's reach. "She called the police, and they called me. Right in the middle of third-period English."

"Oh, damn."

"Mama, the baby can hear you. Do you want that to be the first word he says?"

"Lighten up, darling." Diana pokes my son in the ribs. "You heard it and look how you turned out."

"What's this world coming to if you can't do a neighbor a good turn without getting in trouble with the law? Hand me back that pie, Louise. I'm starving to death."

"Supper's in ten minutes, Aunt Charlotte. I think you'll live till then." Louise hands me the silver, and I start setting the table. "Where's Harry?"

"He's meeting me here."

"I *always* picked Diana up for a date. Any gentleman would."

You might have expected me to be cast in the role of unruly child, but who would have ever dreamed mild-mannered, sweet-tempered Josh would become the stern parent? I'm getting ready to expound on Harry's finer qualities when my cell phone rings.

I race back into the living room and dig around in my purse. As I listen I wish I hadn't heard it ringing. Suddenly all my pizzazz vanishes.

I guess I look as if somebody flattened me with a steamroller because when I go back into the kitchen Josh says, "Mama, what's wrong?"

"Harry can't come. Stomach virus."

Louise and Aunt Charlotte exchange glances that say, Sounds like an excuse to me. Who can blame them? Even I'm having a hard time believing sickness struck two times in a row, just when I want him to meet my family.

Diana puts her arm around me. "Don't worry. We'll meet him next time."

"*Next time* I'll call him, myself," Josh says. "I'm going to meet the man who's taking up all your time, whether he wants to or not."

Diana says, "Shush, darling."

I'm so busy feeling sorry for myself that it takes me a minute to notice Wayne's not there. When I ask about him, Louise explains his business commitment, which sounds bogus to me, but I'd enter that silly bridge tournament Mary Jo's always palavering about before I'd worry her. Just look at her. Lipsticked and pink-cheeked, wearing shorts and sandals instead of her usual Mother Hubbard garb.

"I'd make them pay for standing me up," Aunt Charlotte says. "Now, let's eat before I pass out from hunger."

*Louise*

I know this is awful of me, but while everybody's sitting around the table with coffee and pecan pie, I excuse myself, then sneak into the living room, nab Patsy's purse and shut myself up in the bathroom.

Pressing Call Log I check her last received call and up pops a Denver number. Instead of relief, all I feel is suspicion because obviously Harry used a calling card. Or else he really is in Denver, and either way he has lied to Patsy.

Furthermore, this tells me nothing about Wayne but a lot about myself: I've turned into a sneak. Never mind that Aunt Charlotte would call it good detective work.

If I caught my daughter doing such a thing, I'd think I had failed motherhood. I like to think of myself as a noble, clear-headed woman who always makes good choices. Obviously, you don't really know yourself till you detour off your safe little life's path and get waylaid by push-up bras and sex and a smooth-talking wolf in Italian leather loafers and a Brooks Brothers suit.

Feeling like a toad, I check to see if anybody's looking, then ease out of the bathroom, put Patsy's purse back on the sofa and slink into the kitchen.

"We've saved you some pie." Patsy flashes her brilliant, best-friends smile, and all of a sudden I've lost my appetite for sweets.

From: "The Lady" louisejernigan@yahoo.com
To: "Miss Sass" patsyleslie@hotmail.com
Date: Thursday, October 12, 9:45 p.m.
Subject: My Boyfriend
I started to change the subject because "boy-friend" sounds so silly at my age. Anyhow, I think we need to talk. How does tomorrow night sound to you? Come over and we'll eat leftovers.
XOXO
Louise

From: "Miss Sass" patsyleslie@hotmail.com
To: "The Lady" louisejernigan@yahoo.com
Date: Thursday, October 12, 9:50 p.m.

Subject: Re: My Boyfriend
You don't sound silly at all. I'm just sorry we didn't get to meet each other's honeys tonight.

I was thinking about leaving right after work tomorrow and driving down to Clarksdale for the Cat Head Blues Festival. Why don't you and Aunt Charlotte come? We'll make it a girls' getaway weekend and sit up till all hours gorging on catfish and hush puppies and beer.

XOXOX

Patsy, who can't wait to get out of town


From: "The Lady" louisejernigan@yahoo.com
To: "Miss Sass" patsyleslie@hotmail.com
Date: Thursday, October 12, 9:55 p.m.
Subject: Re: My Boyfriend
I wish I could, but I haven't even seen my cousin Jerry and I need to convince Aunt Charlotte to go home. Not that I don't want her here, but she needs to be with poor old, longsuffering Uncle Bradley. Lord, that man's a saint.

If you go, be careful. Maybe Josh and Diana can go with you. They love blues as much as you do.

XOXOX

Louise

From: "Miss Sass" patsyleslie@hotmail.com
To: "The Lady" louisejernigan@yahoo.com
Date: Thursday, October 12, 10:00 p.m.
Subject: Re: My Boyfriend
Good Lord. Uncle Bradley worships the prickly
pears she walks on. Tell him to take her to Hawaii.
She's been wanting to go.
I'll give Josh and Diana a call. That would be fun.
Just think, I'd have a captive audience while I harp
on Patsy Louise as a name for our granddaughter.
XOXOX
Patsy, who can harp without practice


From: "Miss Sass" patsyleslie@hotmail.com
To: "The Lady" louisejernigan@yahoo.com
Date: Sunday, October 15, 9:40 p.m.
Subject: Blues Festival
I just got back. The festival was great! And of
course we toured the Delta Blues Museum and
had catfish at Morgan Freeman's Grand Zero Blues
Club. What a treat! A young pianist from Greenville
nearly set the keyboard on fire with her boogie-
blues. My favorite song of the entire festival was the
one she does about the woman who slit her "good
man's throat" when she found him cheating. Diana

and I laughed till we cried. I bought her CD. You'll have to come over and hear it.

Is Aunt Charlotte still with you? I didn't see her truck.

XOXOX

Patsy, glad she has a good man who would never cheat

From: "The Lady" louisejernigan@yahoo.com
To: "Miss Sass" patsyleslie@hotmail.com
Date: Sunday, October 15, 9:45 p.m.
Subject: Re: Blues Festival

Diana had already called me to say what a great time the three of you had. I'm glad.

I put a little bee in Uncle Bradley's ear, and he and Jerry drove out Saturday night. Aunt Charlotte wanted to bar the door, till Uncle Bradley held up two plane tickets. "Let that be a lesson, Louise," she told me. "Men love a woman who's a challenge. Settle for chocolate on the little things, but on the big ones, hold out for Hawaii."

It's beginning to feel like fall. I'm making chili tomorrow night. Come over and we'll eat and talk.

XOXOX

Louise

From: "Miss Sass" patsyleslie@hotmail.com
To: "The Lady" louisejernigan@yahoo.com
Date: Sunday, October 15, 9:55 p.m.
Subject: Re: Blues Festival

Can you give me a rain check? I have to go to one of those dreadful bank banquets—you know the kind where the women wear dark business suits, shoes that hurt their feet and fake smiles that look plastered on after three hours of rubber chicken and wilted salad and boring speeches. Tuesday is out, too. Harry's taking me out. He got over his bug, thank goodness!

How about Wednesday? You cook the chili and I'll pick up ice cream.

XOXO

Patsy

P. S. I'm bringing Eden Brent's CD, too. You're going to get such a kick out of that song about the cheating man and the vengeful woman. We can laugh together.

From: "The Lady" louisejernigan@yahoo.com
To: "Miss Sass" patsyleslie@hotmail.com
Date: Sunday, October 15, 10:03 p.m.
Subject: Re: Blues Festival

Wednesday will be great. As soon as you get home from the bank, change into sweats and come on over. I'll have the chili hot.

XOXO

Louise

## CHAPTER 12

*Louise*

I feel like an old fool spying on Patsy, but here I am again taking the low road instead of the high, staked out at the living room window with a pair of opera glasses. Instead of repenting my bad behavior, I'm wishing for bird-watching binoculars. I need a good, strong lens to catch a glimpse of a buzzard.

The kitchen window would give me a better chance of seeing what this old buzzard Harry looks like, but all Patsy has to do is glance my way and she'd see me. In the living room I'm hidden behind the draperies with just a little peephole for my opera glasses.

Where is he? And why am I doing this instead

of stripping off my gardening pants and making a nice salad for supper? Or I could still be out on the front porch repotting the chrysanthemums I bought on the way home from school. There's still enough daylight left. But no, I'm standing here acting like a female version of Inspector Clousseau.

A big Dodge Ram pulls into Patsy's driveway, higher than his low-slung Corvette, which makes it easier to see Harry through the hedge. The truck stops, the door slams and all I see is a dark blur. Frantically I adjust the glasses, but by the time I get a clear picture he has already disappeared into Patsy's house.

Well, shoot. I could have done better without the glasses. All I could tell for sure was that Harry's hair is black like Wayne's. Not much evidence if you're trying to build a case for philandering.

Of course, I'm not trying to build a case. I just want to know the truth, that's all. What I'm hoping is that Harry and Wayne will turn out to be two entirely different men so Patsy can get married and be ridiculously happy. And, of course, I can continue to have a dinner companion who takes care of my need for intelligent male conversation and occasional sex.

Is that too much to ask?

What's keeping Patsy and Harry? I thought she said they were going to Oxford for dinner. I'm getting a cramp in my leg standing sideways in the draperies, and besides that, I have to pee. Do I dare risk running to the toilet? As soon as I do, they'll get in the truck and drive off while I'm flushing and I'll miss another opportunity to find out the truth and stop my own slide into suspicion and skullduggery.

Oh, I feel silly. Why don't I just casually walk over there, knock on Patsy's door and ask to borrow a cup of sugar?

I hurry to the kitchen, jerk open a cabinet door and grab the first cup on the shelf. When the phone rings I jump like somebody caught robbing a 7-Eleven. To make matters worse, the gods of payback time jerk my china teacup out of my hand and smash it against the floor. And it was one of my favorites.

"Hello," I say. "Hello?"

The woman at the other end of the line is carrying on so I can't even tell who it is.

"Patsy, is that you? Slow down. I can't tell a thing you're saying."

"Harry's had a heart attack! You've got to come right over!"

"Call 911. I'll be right there."

Splintered china forgotten, my conscience eased by Patsy's need, I grab my purse, race out the back door, sprint through the hedge and burst into her kitchen. King Kong arches his back and hisses at me. Lord, I feel like hissing back, which just goes to show the ragged state of my nerves.

"Patsy? Where are you?"

She runs through the door, and now I'm the one who nearly has a heart attack. She's wearing majorette boots from high school and a silver sequined skirt that shows off a little bit of neon-pink hot pants and a whole lot of cellulite. And if the pair of pasties with one tassel missing fail to shock ten years off your life, the mussed hair that looks like a bowl of cotton candy will finish the job.

"Oh, Louise." With her mascara streaked from cheekbone to chin, she flings herself on me, sobbing. "We were having a little fun and games before dinner and he started having awful pain."

"Where is he?"

"In my bed."

As we head that way, I ask, "Did you call 911?"

"Yes."

Before I can see Harry, she flings herself across his prone body. This takes a bit of contortion on her part because the mattress is on the floor. Apparently the slats caved in. And not all by themselves, would be my guess.

"Oh, Harry. Don't die."

What if he's already dead?

I skirt around the other side of the bed and there lies Wayne, moaning like somebody's trying to kill him. *That snake.* I want to pick up Patsy's brass lamp and finish him off. I want to stuff his red silk scarves up his nose and keep all oxygen tanks out of reach while he slowly suffocates.

"Quick, Louise. Do CPR!"

I wouldn't touch this double-tongued devil if you gave me the moon with the Milky Way and New York City thrown in for good measure.

Fortunately, I don't have to because the paramedics arrive, and Patsy, who has abandoned all reason, answers the door in her eye-popping getup. The paramedics shoo us out of the way, but not before they get a gander at her ridiculous costume. Even as mad as I am, I grab her raincoat and throw it around her.

"For God's sake, Patsy. Put on some clothes."

"Which one of you is the wife?" one the paramedics says.

"I am," Patsy says. "Or soon will be."

Good Lord. As if it weren't enough that I'm fixing to shatter Patsy's dream, King Kong marches into the room and lets loose a hairball on my shoes.

"Scat!" I swat at him, and he bounds off, leaving me nothing left to do except drop my bombshell. "I doubt that very seriously, Patsy, since the man in your bed is the one I've been dating."

All of a sudden Patsy's looking at me as if I'm on a personal mission to destroy her life and knock off her tomcat with my patent leather purse.

"Louise! How could you!"

I haven't been this mad since she wrecked our

life in New Orleans with the bartender. Wouldn't you think any sane woman would slap Harry Wayne Thompson silly, then kick the two-faced toad out of her bed and into the ambulance? But she has to act like a woman wronged.

For that matter, wouldn't you think I'd go home and say, Good riddance to the two-timing scum dweller?

But *oh, no*. I'm Aunt Charlotte, dead out. Midjudge me and I charge full tilt into battle, even when I know I'm on the wrong battlefield.

So when one of the paramedics says, "Which one of you is going to the hospital to sign admission papers?" I say, "I am."

Patsy glares at me as if I'm Hitler resurrected, then switches her tail in front of me, plops beside the cheating creep and refuses to say another word all the way to the hospital.

Well, what did I expect from the woman who didn't speak to me for a solid year over somebody she didn't even care about? If past experience is any indication, I'll be in the doghouse with Patsy for the next ten years over this perfidious jackass.

When we get to the emergency room both of us bail out behind the gurney, and now there she sits in those silly majorette boots and a raincoat she can't take off even though sweat's running down the side of her face and dripping off her chin. Flipping through out-of-date magazines like there's no tomorrow and she's on a life-or-death mission to discover hairstyles from 1999, she's acting as if I'm contagious and ought to be in quarantine.

I'm not much better off in my gardening pants and flip-flops, fighting the urge to jerk some sense into her by pulling out every peroxided hair on her head. I don't know what I'm doing here in the first place, and even more pressing, I don't know how I'm going to get home.

"Patsy, this is ridiculous."

"I'm not speaking to you."

"Do you realize that neither one of us has a car?"

"I'll call a cab."

"I'm the only one here with a purse."

"If I can't talk a taxi driver into trusting me for the money till I get home, I'll pay with nature's credit card."

I ought to slap her. Instead I go to the vending machines and get myself a cold Diet Pepsi. If she'd behave, I'd get her one, too, but since she's determined to turn this into a family feud, I march right back into the waiting room and proceed to drink my cool Pepsi in front of her.

"Mrs. Leslie?" An intern with blond curls and a face that looks like it ought to be on a Gerber baby food label is standing in the doorway looking at Patsy. "Are you the fiancée?"

"I am." She gives me an arch look as if she's scored the winning point in this asinine game.

"Mr. Thompson's going to be all right. It wasn't a heart attack. It's appendicitis. He's in surgery now."

After he leaves I tell Patsy, "While they're taking out his ruptured appendix, I hope they cut off his lying pecker."

*Patsy*

This is the most humiliating day of my life. Getting caught with your pants down is bad enough, but finding out your best friend betrayed you is the final straw. Louise is smart. Nobody can pull the wool over her eyes. She should have known Wayne Thompson was my Harry.

She needn't sit there with her painted toenails and think I'm going to forget it, either. Because I'm not. For the first time since Rocky died I felt as if I were living my life wide open, full of passion and hope and dreams of a hearth-for-two. I had risen out of a deadening routine and snatched a bright future for myself.

Give me credit. I happen to know that what Harry Wayne was doing was wrong, but once he wakes up I'm sure he'll explain everything. I'm sure he just got caught up in Louise's spell and was planning on letting her down easy but didn't quite know how to do it.

It's easy to get caught in Louise's spell. I did the first day I ever met her. There I was, ten years old, terrified and caring deeply about what everybody thought of me. And there she sat on the front row of Mrs. Beatle's fifth-grade class looking smart and put-together and capable, as if nothing could faze her—not even a new kid with a drunk mother and a daddy who made his living filching the government with bogus workmen's comp claims.

I fell under her charm immediately. I wanted to be her. A part of me has always wanted to be Louise, and when I ran away from New Orleans and lived with Aunt Charlotte, I almost was.

I guess that's one reason I didn't contact her or even speak to her on the phone when she finally found out I was at Aunt Charlotte's. I know I told myself that I didn't want to be a burden to her, that I was glad she had gone all the way to Anchorage to experience life near the frozen tundra. But the truth is, I was almost living her life and I didn't want that to change.

When a nurse comes in to tell us that Harry's surgery is over and we can wait in his room until he's out of recovery, Louise tromps right after her, as if she's the one Harry will want to see first when he wakes up.

Well, I have a news flash for her: I'm going to be the first person Harry sees, and I'll hog the bed to make sure he does. Now that I've become a desirable woman with a fun social life and a scintillating sex life, I'm not fixing to give it all up. Friendship or no friendship.

Of course, no good friend would go off and get a cold Diet Pepsi for herself and drink it right in front of you when you're starving to death, anyway. And she most certainly would not date your man.

Ignoring Louise, I plop myself in the only chair, a great big old lounger by the bed, and she has to lean against the wall with her lipstick and her painted toenails and her new gelled-up hairdo. To think I'm the one who brought her out of her ugly clothes and taught her all about sex appeal. And she used it to lure Harry right from under my nose.

I can't bear to look at her, so I watch the clock instead. The minute hand is inching around so slowly I want to jerk the clock off the wall and stomp it.

After fifteen minutes that feels like fifteen years, Louise speaks.

"So…what are you going to say to him, Patsy?"

"None of your business."

She taps her fingernails on the Pepsi can— trying to drive me stark raving crazy—and marches over to the garbage can like she's got a ramrod up her butt. Her empty can clangs like a cannon—a deliberate, calculated ploy to make me jump.

Then she gives me this *smile*. I'll swear, I never figured Louise for the catty type, but that just shows how wrong you can be about a person, even after forty-five years.

"Well then. I guess I'll be going. Give Harry Wayne my regards."

What I'd like to give him is a little bit of hell, but I figure that will have to wait a while. At least until he gets out of the hospital.

She's hardly out the door before Harry gets wheeled in, groaning and moaning as if he's the only man who ever had his abdomen slit open.

I pat his face and smooth his covers, proving what a caring person I am, in addition to forgiving.

"I'm sorry, Patsy."

His apology doesn't sound genuine to me, but I'm willing to give him the benefit of the doubt. After all, it's not every man who can break the bed slats, land in the middle of the floor and keep on ticking. Which is exactly what Harry did before I lost my tassel and he lost his health.

I pat his hand. "Don't you worry, hon. I'm going to stay right here with you."

## CHAPTER 13

*Louise*

From: "The Lady" louisejernigan@yahoo.com
To: "Miss Sass" patsyleslie@hotmail.com
Date: Tuesday, October17 9:30 p.m.
Subject: Harry Wayne
All the way home in the cab I was thinking how patently ridiculous it is for the two of us to be mad at each other when every bit of this fiasco is Harry Wayne Thompson's fault. I know it was wrong and even mean-spirited of me to drink a Diet Pepsi without offering you a drop, but I swear, Patsy, sometimes you can be so bullheaded I want to slap you.

I know you think I'm culpable in all this, but I didn't know what he was doing any more than you did. After forty-five years you ought to know me better than that. If I couldn't have a man without stealing one from my best friend, I'd do without. And I know you'd do the same.

Besides, we have Josh and Diana to think about. And the baby. For Pete's sake, Patsy, we're family. Call me as soon as you get home. Or send an e-mail if you prefer. Just talk to me. That's all I ask.

Louise

I sit awhile, double-checking the message, then I press Send and go into the kitchen to see if Patsy's home. There are no lights except the one on the front porch that I had the foresight to leave burning.

See. I'm always doing little things like that for her—turning on a light so she won't have to stumble in the dark, making extra soup for her when I cook for Aunt Charlotte, feeding her obstreperous cat and getting her morning papers so they won't pile up on the porch when she has to be out of town.

What I ought to do is get in the car and drive back to the hospital so she'd have a way home. But right now I'm mired in self-righteous indignation and wallowing in fury, and I guess I'm not a big enough person to put all that behind me. Instead

I go to my closet, drag out every rag of clothing I bought to impress that two-timing troglodyte, then dump the whole mess in a garbage bag destined for the Salvation Army and stash it in the garage. I can't stand the stench of mendacity: I am Big Daddy from *Cat on a Hot Tin Roof*.

Next I strip the bed, wash the sheets and put on some that Wayne Thompson has never laid eyes on. On a mission to eradicate him from every nook and cranny, I head to the bathroom to search and destroy. Did he use my hairbrush? There's a telltale black hair. I toss the brush into the wastebasket along with my toothbrush he borrowed. My tube of toothpaste, clean mint flavor, has been squeezed in the middle. I always squeeze from the bottom, so I know he's had his sleazy hands on it. The toothpaste goes into the trash, along with the hand towel he used after he washed his hands.

I feel used, betrayed, dirty even, as if every breath he turned in my direction in the ambulance was contaminated. I turn on the shower and then climb in, clothes and all. As soapy water cascades over my head, down my sweatpants and around my flip-flops I imagine Harry Wayne germs swirling down the drain.

When I'm finally satisfied that every grimy molecule of him is gone, I climb out, strip and march to the washing machine with the soggy clothes, naked as a boiled egg. Then I flip off the lights and storm around my dark house flinging open the windows. Never mind that fall is finally making its chill felt in this Deep South city and rain clouds have blacked out the moon and whipped up a fierce wind.

At last, exhausted, chilled and dripping I go into the kitchen, grab a spoon and eat peanut butter right out of the jar. My hips expand with every bite.

That'll show Patsy and Harry Wayne Thompson.

*Patsy*

I would have stayed longer at the hospital, if for nothing else but to show Louise that Harry belongs to me. But he was asleep and I was sweating like an old nag trying to keep up with a Kentucky Derby Thoroughbred at stud. So I just called a cab.

Now here I am hurtling down my street with

the taxi driver leering at me in the rearview mirror. I had the misfortune of being in a gust of wind just as he drove up to the hospital and he got a good gander at my come-get-me costume. Plus, it's 1:30 a.m. and this town shuts down at midnight. Nobody is on the streets this time of night except hookers or drug dealers.

"My house is next." I act haughty and severe, which is the exact opposite of what I'm feeling. What I want to do is put my head on a soft pillow and bawl like I've lost my last friend. Which I have.

Lord, Lord. Her windows are all wide open and it's fixing to rain and those parquet floors she takes so much pains to wax and polish are going to get wet. In a knee-jerk reaction I reach for my purse to get my cell phone, then I remember I don't have a purse, much less a cell phone, and even if I did I'm not about to call the woman who tried to steal my fiancé.

Let her floors get wet. See if I care.

Finally I get home, and the driver starts to open his door.

"No, just keep your motor running." Immediately I want to bite my tongue off. He's going to think I'm sending him signals. "If you come on the porch my pit bulldog King Kong is liable to burst through the door and tear your head off. I'll be right back with your money."

When I get inside, I find only two dollars in my purse and have to stand on a kitchen chair to get enough money out of the cookie jar on the top shelf to pay the for the cab.

If I fall and break my neck, it will serve Louise right.

*Louise*

Wednesday morning I get up before any self-respecting rooster would dream of stirring and race to the computer to see if Patsy replied to my e-mail. There's nothing in my box except my daily horoscope and six forwards from Mary Jo, which I delete without even reading.

The mailman hasn't even come, so I grind Island Morning Blend from the Java Colony Coffee Company, set it to brewing, then pace between the coffeepot and the window, checking

for signs of life at Patsy's. It would be just like her
to stay at the hospital all night with that fork-
tongued jerk.

I'm on my second cup of coffee—a rare luxury
for me on a school day—when I hear the postman.
On the porch I try to catch a glimpse of life at
Patsy's but I'm thwarted by the hedge that bushed
out overnight just to spite me. To top it all off, my
only piece of mail is a postcard from Aunt Charlotte in Kauai bearing this cryptic message: "I'm
fixing to dump Bradley in the Wailua River and
come home. He can spend the rest of his days in
the Fern Grotto for all I care."

Lord, Lord. My aunt's fixing to kill my uncle,
my best friend hates the quicksand I walk on and
our children will have a conniption fit when they
find out I was dating Patsy's boyfriend. Or she was
dating mine. Take your pick.

If I didn't know Mercury is in retrograde, I'd go
inside and hang myself with the coffeepot cord. As
it is, I console myself that the disruption of order
in my life is not my fault; it's all due to cosmic dis-
turbances. And I don't feel a bit guilty placing

blame elsewhere, either. I go to church on Sunday, tithe when the offering plate comes around and carry a travel toothbrush in my purse so I can brush after every meal. I'm a good woman trying to do the right thing.

With one small exception, my ill-advised fling with Harry Wayne, I've never deviated from the right path. But now that I've thrown away my push-up bras and sworn off scoundrels and Lycra, I'm hoping my life will get back to normal.

I dress in plain polyester and loafers, then climb into my car. Patsy's kitchen light flips on, and I bail out, race to her back door and knock.

"Patsy. I know you're in there. Open up."

The only response is from King Kong, who jumps on the windowsill and spits at me. I pound the door and rattle the latched screen, but Patsy ignores me. I hope King Kong spits a hairball on her majorette boots.

The only explanation I can give for heading to the hospital after school is temporary loss of sanity. Naturally I'm telling myself that I'm going to have it out with Harry Wayne and find out exactly why he squired around both of us so I can set Patsy free with the truth.

The elevators seem stuck on the third floor, so finally I huff up two flights of stairs. On the top landing I have to bend over and heave awhile before I can get my breath. Instead of visiting Harry Wayne I ought to be sweating on the stationary bicycle I keep in my closet for inspiration. So far, the only thing it inspires in me is perspiration, and I'm usually not in the mood to sweat.

When I finally get the starch back in my legs, I totter down to room 216 and ease through the door. He's asleep with his mouth open. Not a pretty picture. Especially without teeth. His dentures are in a cup by his bed. One of the many things I didn't know about Harry Wayne Thompson.

Beside his dentures are Tums and a tube of Preparation H. Two more things I didn't know—hemorrhoids and acid reflux. Serves the old goat right.

Sitting in the room's only chair, I breathe awhile till I'm feeling normal again, then I reach for the only reading material in the room—a daily devotional book probably left by a group of generous-hearted little old ladies from Trinity Baptist.

Harry Wayne has obviously taken their visit to heart because when he opens one bloodshot eye and sees me, he scrambles around for his dentures. I hope they fall on the floor and break.

They don't, of course, since real life is not like the movies where jerks get their comeuppance with some regularity and perfect cinematic timing.

"Hello, Louise. How are you?"

He acts as if this is any ordinary Wednesday and I've come to talk to him about the weather.

It seems prophetic to me that the daily devotional is open to a section warning of the sins of fornication.

"I'm quite well for a woman who betrayed her best friend with a sick old goat who couldn't keep his pants zipped."

"Now, babe…"

"Don't you 'now babe' me. You might be able to sweet-talk your way around Patsy, but you don't fool me. Did you think you would get away with dating both of us?"

"I didn't mean for it to happen."

"If you say 'The devil made me do it,' I'm going to hit you over the head with your bedpan."

"One of the reasons I like you so much is that you call a spade a spade."

"Harry Wayne, I don't give a flying flip whether you like me or not. All I want to know is, why did you do such a thing and what do you plan to do about Patsy?"

"What do you mean, 'What do you plan to do about Patsy?'"

Patsy sweeps through the door in three-inch heels and a three-inch skirt. She's fixing to break her fool neck and expose her peach blossom to the young male nurse who is right behind her.

"You Jezebel," she adds. "Get out of Harry's room."

"Now, Patsy, wait a minute. I didn't mean what you thought you heard." *Oh, help*.

The nurse clears his throat. "Now, ladies…"

"My hearing's perfectly intact, thank you very much. But if you don't move your butt, your hair won't be because I'm fixing to yank it out by the roots."

"Please, ladies. We've got a very sick man in here."

I've never been one to create a public scene, so I put the daily devotional in the chair—deliberately leaving it open to the section on fornication—then exit with as much dignity as I can under the circumstances; meaning that I hang on to my bladder till I round the corner and sprint toward the bathroom. This is one of my most embarrassing qualities: every time I'm excited, tickled or under stress, I have to pee.

Wouldn't you know the elevator is now working? Since going down is always easier than coming up, I view this reversal as a deliberate calculation to put a rotten cherry on the melted ice-cream sundae of my day.

*Patsy*

From: "The Lady" louisejernigan@yahoo.com
To: "Miss Sass" patsyleslie@hotmail.com
Date: Wednesday, October 18, 6:00 p.m.
Subject: Truce

Listen, Patsy. This is ridiculous. I'm not after Harry
Wayne Thompson. If he disappeared down a hole
all the way to China, I wouldn't give a flying flitter.
Let's call a truce and try to get back to normal.

We can start with quilting tomorrow night. I'm
sure Betty Lynn and Mary Jo will be glad to see
us. I'll pick you up or you can pick me up. I know
how you hate my driving.

But please, please, for Pete's sake, stop hating me.
I didn't do a thing except go out with a man I had
no inkling was the same one you were dating.

Louise, who really and truly is your friend

The nerve of her. The gall. I wouldn't be caught
in the same room with her if you tried to bribe me
with a six-carat diamond ring. I'm so mad I haul
off and send a reply before I can gather my wits.

From: "Miss Sass" patsyleslie@hotmail.com
To: "The Lady" louisejernigan@yahoo.com
Date: Wednesday, October 18, 9:00 p.m.
Subject: Re: Truce
As far as I'm concerned you can stick that white flag
where it doesn't snow. And you can forget about
me going to quilting with you. You go this Thursday

and I'll go next. Or vice versa. I don't care as long as I don't have to be in the same room with you. Furthermore, I'm telling Josh not to expect me for Sunday dinner. I'm not about to put my feet under the same table as you. You might as well count me out when it comes your turn to cook, too. The way you've been acting, I'm afraid you'd put arsenic in my coffee.

And don't even think about slinking through the hedge when my turn for Sunday dinner rolls around. If you do I'll sic King Kong on your butt.

Patsy

P.S. Did I ever tell you how silly I think it is to waste money on gourmet coffee beans when Folgers Instant will do just as well? After all these years you could have saved enough to buy a ticket to Paris to buy some real French perfume.

From: "The Lady" louisejernigan@yahoo.com
To: "Miss Sass" patsyleslie@hotmail.com
Date: Wednesday, October 18, 9:10 p.m.
Subject: Re: Truce

How ridiculous of you to talk about flying to Paris for French perfume when you could see the Mona Lisa and the Eiffel Tower and the Arc de Triomphe.

But at least you're talking to me.

Fine. I'll take quilting this Thursday and you take it next. I'll tell Mary Jo and Betty Lynn we have twin mystery viruses that strike and recede then recur on alternate weeks.

I don't know what you're going to tell Josh and Diana about not coming to Sunday dinner, but don't expect me to make up any excuses for you. In fact, don't expect me to ever again dignify your bad behavior with a genteel lie.

Louise, who has had it

From: "Miss Sass" patsyleslie@hotmail.com
To: "The Lady" louisejernigan@yahoo.com
Date: Wednesday, October 18, 9:15 p.m.
Subject: Re: Truce

Fine. Be that way. See if I care.

Patsy, wronged and pissed

I turn my laptop off, then slam the lid shut. I'm not fixing to check my e-mail for the next ten years. That's the only way I'll ever keep myself from speaking to that man-stealing Jezebel on the other side of the hedge.

And while I'm burning fences I might as well call Josh and tell him not to expect me to ever eat at the same table as Louise. If I catch him before the ten-o'clock news, he'll be more receptive to my situation.

When he answers the phone, I get right to the point. "I'm not coming to Sunday dinner."

"What's wrong, Mama? Are you sick?"

"In a manner of speaking."

"That tells me exactly nothing. What's the problem?"

Suddenly I'm wishing I hadn't leaped before I looked. There's no way I can tell him about Louise without upsetting Diana, and I'd let King Kong claw the leather upholstery in my Jag before I'd hurt my darling daughter-in-law. I don't know how I ever got lucky enough to have her in the first place.

Well, I do, of course. Having Diana in the family was Josh's doing, not mine. Everything he does is perfect, even if I am his mother.

And, of course, if I upset Diana, Josh will be furious at me.

"It's Harry," I say. "He's in the hospital and I'm the only one he has to take care of him."

"We'll miss you, Mama. Give my love to Mama Two."

What can I say but okay? I feel like I've just flushed my best diamond down the toilet. Here I am lying to my own son. If I'm to keep the peace with him and Diana, it will be the first of many lies.

I just won't think about it. That's all.

In the bathroom I smear makeup remover on my face, and all of a sudden I'm crying, not sweet ladylike sniffles, but heaving sobs and nose-reddening snorts and big tears that leave crooked paths through the cream. My eyes are going to swell up like toad frogs.

"Oh, Rocky. What am I going to do now?"

I used to fancy I could hear his replies when I asked these questions, but why should I expect him to answer me now? A foolish old woman with her brain between her legs.

For the past forty-five years, the one constant in my life has been my friendship with Louise, and now it's gone, swept away in my attempt to find somebody to love. Louise will be all right. She always is. She'll fall back on her books, her career at the high school, her church and her active civic life.

But what do I have to fall back on? TV talk shows where self-styled experts are telling me one minute to take care of my physical needs, never mind age, and the next they're saying get in touch with my inner self, go off to a mountain somewhere in Nepal and contemplate my navel.

I see my navel every day when I bathe, and so far I can't tell that the sight has done a thing for me except drive me to order one of those foolish contraptions called an ab cruncher on QVC.

Louise is probably standing on her back porch gazing at the stars and having lofty thoughts about the nature of the universe. I've seen her there many an evening, still and peaceful, her face lifted and shining as if she knows cosmic secrets. Once I asked her about it and she said, "Patsy, we're all connected. The stars, the sun, the moon, everything in the heavens and in the earth below. When I see the grandeur and order of the night skies, I'm reminded that I'm just a tiny piece of a vast whole. And that gives me comfort. I'm fallible, human, allowed to make mistakes, to repent, to learn and hopefully to grow."

I used to wish I could be just like her, wise and brave and good. Or so I thought.

That just goes to show that you don't really know another person until both of you fall for the same man.

Thinking of Harry, I stop crying and wash my face.

I may have lost Louise, but I still have Harry. Oh, I know he's not perfect. But then, neither am I. If we can get through this little hitch in our relationship, we'll be fine. After I'm married, I might even forgive Louise.

## Louise

It was bad enough when Mary Jo and Betty Lynn plied me with questions about Patsy, but when my own daughter asks, "Do you think we ought to send flowers to Harry?" I want to tell her, Send bonbons laced with arsenic.

The chicken casserole she and Josh made for

Sunday dinner turns to sawdust. Finally I tell her, "No, you don't even know him."

"Mama seems serious," Josh says. "Maybe I ought to go to the hospital and get to know him."

*Lord*, I wish I were Solomon. I can't tell them what happened without splitting this family wide open. Instead I change the subject.

"Aunt Charlotte and Uncle Bradley are coming home next Friday."

"Is she behaving?"

Nobody in my life is behaving. Diana's astute and so is Josh. If Patsy and I don't settle our mess it won't take them long to see through us.

"No, she threatened to come home and leave him in the Fern Grotto when he said he wouldn't take her to Waimea Canyon."

"Why wouldn't he go?" Josh says. "It's really spectacular."

"Think about it, darling." Diana smiles at her husband, and I say a silent prayer that they will always be this way. "Would you go with Aunt Charlotte? She'd leave the beaten path and go sprinting off somewhere and break her neck."

"That's exactly what Uncle Bradley told her,"
I say.

"Should I be worried?" Josh makes a mock-
horror face. "Does this kind of bullheadedness run
in the family?"

"If it does, Patsy Louise will be a holy terror."

I'm thinking of Patsy when I say this, and not
Aunt Charlotte. Of course, I'm also thinking of a
new name for my granddaughter. Diana Louise. It
has a very nice ring.

It might even make Patsy come to her senses,
if she has any left. I can tell you one thing: I don't
intend to keep prodding her with e-mails to find
out. She's a grown woman. Let her act like one.

CHAPTER 14

*Patsy*

**It's** been more than a week since Harry got home from the hospital, and I'm still waiting for him to explain why he dated my best friend. I'm on the way to his apartment now with three kinds of salad I got from Finney's Sandwich Shop—chicken, tuna and potato which I switched to my own platter.

If Harry thinks I'm a wonderful cook it might speed up his apology and my determined march to the altar. I'm idling at a red light thinking how impressed he's going to be when Josh calls on my cell. Even before I answer, I know what my son is going to say.

"Hey, Josh. What's up?"

"Mama, who are you trying to fool with your nonchalant act? You didn't come to Sunday dinner at our house and you didn't show up at Mama Two's. What's going on?"

"You know I'm still taking care of Harry."

"You've never put your family last. And Mama Two seems distracted. Diana's worried, and I don't like to worry her, especially this close to delivery."

"I don't want to worry her, hon. Tell her I'll see her at my house Sunday."

"Will Mama Two be there?"

There's no way to answer that without adding fuel to his fire, so I pretend I'm losing my phone signal.

"What? What's that? I can't hear you. Talk later. 'Bye."

It will be a relief to walk into Harry's apartment and have nothing to do except eat chicken salad and have him admire my new hot-pink, spike-heeled shoes. I let myself in with my very own key.

If Louise knew he gave it to me, it would show her once and for all who is in charge of Harry Wayne Thompson's heart. But I haven't heard from her since she sent me that tacky e-mail about her telling "genteel" lies for me, or some such garbage.

Well, fine. Let her act that way. See if I send her an invitation to my wedding.

"Is that you, babe?" He's calling from the bedroom where the radio is playing Elvis's version of "I Need Your Love Tonight." I take the song personally.

"It's me, honey bun."

It's nice to have somebody greet me with a term of endearment, even if it is one I used to despise. "Babe" grows on you.

I set the salad platter in his small kitchenette, fluff my hair and add extra gloss to my lips, just in case. Harry's doing so well I expect any day we can resume our regular activities, if you know what I mean.

The curtains are drawn, only a small lamp glows—a good sign since it's only seven o'clock. Plus, he's already in bed. A very good sign.

"I thought you'd never get here. I'm dying of thirst and my hemorrhoids are killing me. Can you get me a glass of water and while you're at it, get the Preparation H."

Of all the nerve. What's he doing in bed acting like an invalid? Why, his incision is hardly bigger than my thumb. They do that now with appendicitis—cut this little bitty place you wouldn't think they could get a pencil through, much less a body organ.

Here I am in killer-pink designer shoes expecting compliments and kisses and what do I get? A request for hemorrhoid suppositories.

I'm so mad I could stomp grapes. Without a word I march into the bathroom, grab a tube and hand it to him.

"Here you go, Harry. While you tend to your aches and pains I'll see about your water."

In the kitchen I get a glass and then just stand their waiting. And smiling. Before long I hear what I'm listening for.

"Owww…Ouch! What the hell?"

I move to the hallway and watch him hotfoot toward the bathroom, turn on the water and try to heft his bare bottom into the lavatory. Then I walk calmly back into the kitchen and pour him a glass of water.

"Here you go, hon."

"Patsy…my God." He takes big gulps of water. "What did you give me?"

"Why? What's the matter?"

"I'm on fire, that's what."

"Oh, dear." I go back to the bed, pick up the tube and put on such a horrified look you'd think I had lost my best friend. Which I have.

"What?" he yells. "What is it?"

"Oh, Harry. I'm soooo sorry. It's Ben-Gay, Icy Hot."

That'll teach him to treat me like a nurse. Furthermore, he's not a pretty sight with his butt in the sink. I'm losing interest in impressing him with Finney's chicken salad.

When I get home, wouldn't you know there'd be an e-mail from Louise? It's bad enough that my chicken salad and pink shoes went to waste. Now I have to put up with another preachy "why don't you act right?" message from my former best friend.

What I ought to do is just delete it, but curiosity gets the best of me.

From: "The Lady" louisejernigan@yahoo.com
To: "Miss Sass" patsyleslie@hotmail.com
Date: Friday, October 27, 7:00 p.m.
Subject: Sunday dinner at your house
I haven't told the kids about our silly spat over that despicable dirt bag, and thank God it looks as if you haven't, either. So that leaves us with another Sunday dinner to lie about. Do you have any suggestions? I don't know how much longer we're going to be able to keep up this charade without Josh and Diana guessing the truth.
Louise
P. S. When you are going to get your head out of the clouds and see Harry Wayne for the two-timing toad he is? He won't hold a candle to Rocky Delgado.

From: "Miss Sass" patsyleslie@hotmail.com
To: "The Lady" louisejernigan@yahoo.com
Date: Friday, October 27, 9:00 p.m.
Subject: Re: Sunday dinner at your house
You leave Rocky out of this. And if you don't quit calling Harry ugly names I'm going to turn King Kong loose in that chrysanthemum bed you're so proud of. As for Sunday dinner, I don't care what

you tell the kids as long as you don't darken my door.

Patsy

P.S. I think you ought to name yourself something besides "The Lady." You've fallen so far from that pedestal it would take a forty-foot crane to get you back up.

From: "The Lady" louisejernigan@yahoo.com
To: "Miss Sass" patsyleslie@hotmail.com
Date: Friday, October 27, 9:10 p.m.
Subject: Re: Sunday dinner at your house

Do you realize we're acting like a couple of hormone-driven teenagers? My Lord, Patsy, we're almost old enough for Social Security. If you want that old turd you can have him. Just quit acting like I'm your enemy. I'm not.

Louise

From: "Miss Sass" patsyleslie@hotmail.com
To: "The Lady" louisejernigan@yahoo.com
Date: Friday, October 27, 9:15 p.m.
Subject: Re: Sunday dinner at your house

Like he's yours to give? For your information, I already have Harry. And as long as you keep

acting the way you are about him, you're certainly not welcome around me.
Patsy

From: "The Lady" louisejernigan@yahoo.com
To: "Miss Sass" patsyleslie@hotmail.com
Date: Friday, October 27, 9:20 p.m.
Subject: Re: Sunday dinner at your house
I give up. Let's just stick to the point. Okay? I'll tell Diana and Josh I have to drive out to the farm to see about Aunt Charlotte and Uncle Bradley. Nobody will doubt that. I just want to make sure we get our stories straight.
Louise

From: "Miss Sass" patsyleslie@hotmail.com
To: "The Lady" louisejernigan@yahoo.com
Date: Friday, October 27, 9:26 p.m.
Subject: Re: Sunday dinner at your house
Fine.
Patsy

I turn off the computer and march to the kitchen in my new pink shoes. Actually, I wobble. Lord, they're not making four-inch heels as steady as they once did. I used to wear them all day long without so much as a twinge. Now they're killing me. I unfasten the ankle straps and kick the shoes off, then go to the table and remove the Saran wrap from the rest of my Finney's salads.

Ordinarily I'd have stored the leftovers in Harry's refrigerator, but since he had to act like some old fart, I brought the leftovers home.

Now I'm glad I did. I get a fork and eat right off the platter. Standing up.

I don't know when I've enjoyed food so much. Since I met Harry I've been picking at my meals like one of those starved-looking models who, once you take off their makeup, look like boys.

I clean the platter and wish I had some more. I wish I could pick up the phone and call Louise and say, Come over and bring chocolate cherry cake. We'd sit in the middle of my bed and giggle like teenagers.

Was she right? Am I acting like a hormone-driven teenager over Harry? And do I have my head in the clouds?

The fact is, he *did* lie to me. More than once. And he *knew* Louise was my best friend because he'd seen her picture on my dresser. We'd talked about her.

So what if she's not the only one? What if I was his Tuesday woman and Louise was his Thursday woman and he had two or three more stashed away for Monday, Wednesday and Friday?

Oh, I can't let myself get bushwhacked with that kind of negative thinking. If I do, I'll end up back in the same old rut: bridge and quilting and the bank without nothing in between except an endless stretch of days where the most uplifting thing I do is paint my toenails purple.

Leaving the pink shoes under the table, I rinse the platter, put it in the dishwasher and then go into the bathroom to take off my makeup.

Good God, is that me in the mirror? I look like a clown, a buffoon, a fifty-five-year-old woman trying to pretend she's twenty. Maybe it's time to ditch the Marilyn Monroe vamp and go for a softer look.

While I'm at it, I might as well give the pink shoes to Goodwill. And the red ones that look just like them. No man is worth swollen feet and cramping legs. Not even Harry.

*Especially* not Harry.

## Louise

As soon as Sunday services are over I drive straight to the farm so I won't run into Josh and Diana at Patsy's. My daughter was suspicious when I said I had to skip Sunday dinner, and I don't want to subject myself to further questioning.

Lord. I alternate between wanting to shake some sense into Patsy and wanting to race through the hedge, sit at her kitchen table and tell her every little detail of my day. When we were living in New Orleans and juggling my day shift with her night shift, we had only fifteen minutes in between to catch up. We learned how to pare the details down to the bare bones, how to get straight to the heart of a matter without exposition.

During the year I was in Alaska and she was staying with Aunt Charlotte, that's what I missed most—our private sessions where we learned to expose our souls in three minutes or less. We called them power chats, and now I don't know if I'll have another one with Patsy.

I don't have time to dwell on the subject because Aunt Charlotte meets me in the front yard. Here it comes. More bad news.

"Louise, you've got to see this." She grabs my hand before I'm even out of the car.

"Hold on, Aunt Charlotte. I'm not as spry as I once was."

"Piffle. That's your own durned fault. You ought to be out here on the farm running up and down these hills instead of sitting on your behind quilting and shuffling a bunch of silly cards."

She comes to an abrupt halt, and I've been moving forward at such a pace I almost fall flat on my face. Wouldn't that be the curdled cream in the cheap coffee of my day? A broken hip.

"Look over yonder." She points to a brand-new John Deere Gator utility vehicle with a tilting cargo box attached to the back. "It's a bribe from Bradley."

Aunt Charlotte loves to keep you in suspense, so I can't decide if this is good news or bad, but

I'm bound and determined to put a bright spin on it. I'm so tired of turmoil I could curl into the sweet-smelling Bermuda grass at my feet and sleep for sixteen hours.

"It's a splendid gift. By the way, where is Uncle Bradley?"

"Off playing golf with Fred Winkler." She runs her hands over the John Deere's hood. "It's a dandy all right. It's even got a power lift for the cargo box."

She hops on to demonstrate, looking as natural as the stand of black-eyed Susans growing in the nearby pasture. In spite of her age and the danger she poses to herself and anybody in her path when she's riding her tractor, Aunt Charlotte belongs on the famous green farm equipment.

"He said I could have it on one condition."

"What was that?"

"I had to give him my keys and promise not to pester him again about my tractor."

Smart man. He has struck the perfect compromise, downsizing from a huge tractor to the smaller, more manageable four-wheeler.

"Did you?"

"Not till I kept him guessing a few hours."

"Poor Uncle Bradley. You should be easier on him."

"Piffle. If I didn't keep him on his toes, he'd shrivel up and die. A little piss and vinegar keeps you young."

"You wouldn't happen to have any on hand, would you? I feel two hundred years old."

"I bet it's over that old Harry Wayne character. You never did tell me what you found out, and I prissed off to Hawaii and forgot all about it."

"You should forget it. There's no use worrying you with my problems."

"Piffle. That's what families are for. Are you going to tell me or do I have to pry it out of you?"

She leads me to the courtyard she designed so you'd think you were in Italy. Underneath a replica of Michelangelo's David she had shipped over from Florence, I bring Aunt Charlotte up-to-date on the Harry Wayne saga.

Telling it aloud allows me to see exactly how foolish the story is.

"I know it sounds like an episode of *As the World Turns*."

"More like As the Worm Turns. I've never heard of anything as asinine in all my life. Patsy knows better than to stay moony-eyed over a two-timing man, and so do you."

I don't make excuses, because my part in this silly business is indefensible. Why did I blurt out the truth while Patsy was beside herself? And why did I crawl into that ambulance instead of going back home and giving her time to recover from the shock of practically killing that horny toad with sex?

More to the point, why did I go out with a man I hardly knew in the first place?

"I lost the stars in my eyes the minute I found him in her bed. But I'm afraid Patsy fancies herself in the middle of a great love story. I don't know how in the world to get this mess straightened out. The way things are going, we'll have to take turns visiting the baby, and Josh and Diana will have to have two christenings."

"Leave it to me. I'll fix things."

The idea of leaving things to Aunt Charlotte

makes me sweat even though it's a brisk sixty degrees and I'm wearing a wool-blend sweater set. A vision of her on Patsy's front porch breaking federal law comes to mind.

"No, thank you, Aunt Charlotte. I'll figure it out. But at this point, Patsy and I will never get back together without an Act of Congress or an act of God."

"Well, Mother, you might as well consider this Divine Intervention."

Diana is standing in the French doors leading from the den to the courtyard, and if calling me "Mother" instead of "Mom" isn't enough to tip me off, her face is. I've seen that thunderous expression only a few times in her life, and when I do I usually dive for cover. Diana is not easy to rile, but when you get her stirred up you don't want to be any closer than the next county.

"How much did you hear?"

"Not as much as I intend to." She kisses Aunt Charlotte on the cheek. "The front door was unlocked and I saw Mother's car and just came on inside. I hope you don't mind."

"Don't be silly. Have I ever?"

She sits heavily in a padded rocking chair then smoothes her maternity top over her enormous belly. There's such tenderness and beauty in the way she caresses her unborn child I want to fall on my knees and weep.

*Please*, I'm thinking. Just that. *Please*.

This is everything, this circle of family and friends, unbroken until now. And I will do everything in my power to heal the breach. I must.

"What did Patsy tell you?"

"Nothing yet. But Josh stayed there to find out."

In spite of the cool temperatures, she fans herself with her hands and Aunt Charlotte hops up.

"I'll get us some cold Pepsis. Don't say a thing till I get back."

"What tipped you off?" I ask my daughter.

"Mother, did you think you could keep avoiding each other without raising our suspicions? My gosh, the two of you have been inseparable for years. It didn't take us long to guess that something is seriously wrong."

"That piss ant they've both been dating. That's

what's wrong." Aunt Charlotte plops Pepsis in front of us, the condensation rolling down the sides of the cool cans. "Any fool knows if you put two hens and one rooster in the henhouse together, feathers will fly. They've been dating the same old rooster."

"My Lord…" Diana looks pale, and I'm so mad I could eat oysters with a splinter.

"Aunt Charlotte, you didn't have to blurt it out like that."

"Somebody had to."

"Look, Diana, it's going to take a while to straighten this out. Patsy's still serious about Harry, and quite frankly, I don't have a clue how to get through to her."

"Well, Mother, you'd better think of something quick, because neither one of you is welcome at my house until the two of you have patched things up. I'm not taking sides, I'm not making visitation schedules, and I'm most certainly not going to bring this baby into the world in the midst of a family squabble."

There she sits—my act of God. Now if I can

only conjure the wisdom of Solomon, I might be able to put things right with Patsy. Until then all I know to do is drink my Pepsi and pray.

## CHAPTER 15

*Patsy*

**Where's** the man who broke the bed slats? That's what I want to know. Here I am in Harry's bedroom trying to recapture the old magic, and the only body part that's tingling is my left arm where he's got it pinned under his elbow.

Of course, how can you expect to shoot the moon after your son rakes you over the coals, your daughter-in-law has decreed no more Sunday dinners and your former best friend has turned Aunt Charlotte on you?

She called right after Josh left and said, "Patsy, if you and Louise don't straighten out this mess over that shiftless man, I'm going to quit speaking to either one of you." I told her, "Aunt Charlotte, it's not my fault," and she said, "I don't care whose fault it is, just fix it before I have to."

I came straight to Harry's, hoping to forget my problems by resurrecting a miracle. So far, all I've resurrected is a twinge of guilt and hardly enough passion to make a spit ball. It's a relief when the doorbell rings.

"I'll get it," I say, then leap up, jerk on my clothes and walk out while Harry's still saying, "Just ignore it, babe."

A delivery boy from Betty's Beautiful Bouquets says, "Flowers for Harry Wayne Thompson."

Well, I most certainly did not select these tacky red carnations, and you'd think Louise would have better taste. The minute the delivery boy leaves I check the card. "Gloria," it reads, which lets Louise off the hook but opens another whole can of worms.

"Who was it, toots?"

Harry's standing by the recliner with his hair a mess and his shirt buttoned wrong. He looks like a washed-up Romeo.

I wave the flowers at him. "Who's Gloria?"

"My secretary. From the office. She sends flowers to everybody who gets sick. It's part of her job."

The more he talks the more he looks like a jaded Don Juan whose goose just got cooked. I'm so mad I could whack him over the head with his cheap carnations.

Tomorrow I'm going to pay a visit to the tasteless Gloria. At one time or another, practically everybody at City Hall has been at my teller's window with paychecks and one-minute synopses of their terrible/wonderful day. Take your pick. It won't be hard for me to find this inelegant Gloria creature.

"How sweet," I tell him, meaning exactly the opposite. "It's been fun, hon."

I peck him on the cheek and hand him the flowers. Let him get his own vase.

From: "The Lady" louisejernigan@yahoo.com
To: "Miss Sass" patsyleslie@hotmail.com
Date: Sunday, October 29, 5:00 p.m.
Subject: Our children
By now I'm sure you are aware that our children know. We can't keep this up, Patsy. When you get

this message, come over and let's talk. I'll be home all evening.

Louise, holding out an olive branch


From: "Miss Sass" patsyleslie@hotmail.com
To: "The Lady" louisejernigan@yahoo.com
Date: Sunday, October 29, 7:30 p.m.
Subject: Re: Our children

I don't know what you and Aunt Charlotte told Diana to make her angry enough to cancel Sunday dinners, but thanks to you, my daughter-in-law now hates me.

Patsy


From: "The Lady" louisejernigan@yahoo.com
To: "Miss Sass" patsyleslie@hotmail.com
Date: Sunday, October 29, 7:35 p.m.
Subject: Re: Our children

My daughter *does not* hate you. That's not in her nature. Her hormones are running amok and she overreacted, that's all. Besides, you should have known she'd be upset when she found out we're not even on speaking terms. What did Josh have to say?

Louise, offering chocolate cherry cake in addition to the olive branch

From: "Miss Sass" patsyleslie@hotmail.com
To: "The Lady" louisejernigan@yahoo.com
Date: Sunday, October 29, 7:40 p.m.
Subject: Re: Our children
Are you trying to bribe me? It won't work. I'm still
mad at you.
You know Josh. He never gets riled. After he dug
the truth out of me, he just said, "Fix it, Mama."
I don't know how I'm supposed to do that when I
wasn't the one who broke it.
Patsy

From: "The Lady" louisejernigan@yahoo.com
To: "Miss Sass" patsyleslie@hotmail.com
Date: Sunday, October 29, 7:45 p.m.
Subject: Re: Our children
Well, *I* certainly didn't break it. When are you
going to get your head out of the clouds and turn
your anger on the real culprit? That's all I'm saying
on the subject.
Louise, wanting to take the olive branch and
whip your fanny

From: "Miss Sass" patsyleslie@hotmail.com
To: "The Lady" louisejernigan@yahoo.com

Date: Sunday, October 29, 7:48 p.m.
Subject: Re: Our children
Good. Don't say another word.
By the way, did Harry ever go limp in midclinch with you?
Patsy, just wondering


From: "The Lady" louisejernigan@yahoo.com
To: "Miss Sass" patsyleslie@hotmail.com
Date: Sunday, October 29, 7:53 p.m.
Subject: Re: Our children
No, but he used to belch and pretend it was a hiccup.
Louise


From: "Miss Sass" patsyleslie@hotmail.com
To: "The Lady" louisejernigan@yahoo.com
Date: Sunday, October 29, 8:00 p.m.
Subject: Re: Our children
One time I told him I loved Puccini and he said he'd never understood women's fondness for designer handbags.
Patsy


From: "The Lady" louisejernigan@yahoo.com
To: "Miss Sass" patsyleslie@hotmail.com

Date: Sunday, October 29, 8:04 p.m.
Subject: Re: Our children
You should have mentioned cars instead of opera.
Once I told him that I thought Portia was a great
character, and he said, "I don't know how much
character she has, but she's a damned fine car."
For goodness sake, he's an engineer. Wouldn't
you think he had heard of Shakespeare?
Louise

From: "Miss Sass" patsyleslie@hotmail.com
To: "The Lady" louisejernigan@yahoo.com
Date: Sunday, October 29, 8:10 p.m.
Subject: Re: Our children
If he did, he probably thought it was some kind
of sword. Besides, I'm having my doubts about
Harry Wayne being an engineer. That's the story
he told you. He told me he was the planner for the
city's Fairpark District.
Patsy
P.S. I didn't know you admired Portia that much.

From: "The Lady" louisejernigan@yahoo.com
To: "Miss Sass" patsyleslie@hotmail.com
Date: Sunday, October 29, 8:15 p.m.

Subject: Re: Our children
Exactly. Harry Wayne was never straightforward with either one of us. What other lies do you think we'd discover if we started digging?
Louise
P.S. I admire her as one of Shakespeare's characters. Where Portia and I part company is over her speech, "Ay me, how weak a thing the heart of woman is!" I happen to think the heart of woman is so fierce and courageous it can break a thousand times and come back stronger than ever. Listen, Patsy, when Rocky died and your heart crumbled, you battled poverty and single-motherhood and a soul-stealing job in a two-bit bar to put it back together. Don't you dare let the likes of Harry Wayne Thompson break you.

From: "Miss Sass" patsyleslie@hotmail.com
To: "The Lady" louisejernigan@yahoo.com
Date: Sunday, October 29, 8:30 p.m.
Subject: Re: Our children
I don't think I can handle any more pep talks today, and I never was as good as you at soul searching. I'm going to bed.
Patsy, pooped

*Louise*

Last night's e-mails to Patsy didn't solve the problem, but they cracked open the door. That's what I'm thinking as I check my box at school for mail. There's a note from the principal asking me to come to his office.

Give John Cramer a red suit and he could play Santa Claus without benefit of makeup. Even his personality matches. Jovial and kind, he looks like the kind of man who would give you anything you asked for if he had a workshop full of elves and eight tiny reindeer.

"Sit down, Louise." His eyes twinkle when I walk into his office. "I guess you know what this is about."

"The Christmas dance." I've been the senior sponsor for this annual holiday event for the last ten years. "I think you need a fresh perspective, Dr. Cramer. Somebody younger than I. Laura Laney from the math department would be a good choice."

"You've always done a splendid job, but if you need a break, I'll understand."

"In a few weeks I'll have my first grandbaby."

Jennifer West, who sponsors the cheerleaders, has two grandchildren. If you told her she was too old she'd laugh and do a cartwheel. Of course, she does Pilates and has had gymnastic training. Still, I don't know how she keeps her enthusiasm.

Is that what I was doing in Harry Wayne Thompson's bed? Trying to fill an empty place Roy left behind? Trying to rekindle a spark I used to feel every time I walked into the classroom? Trying to recapture my spirit and invent a new dream?

Now Dr. Cramer says to me, "Why don't you give it some thought, Louise? Take your time. I don't have to appoint anyone for a couple of weeks."

By the time my fifth-period class, senior English, rolls around, the school grapevine has spread news that I'm not going to sponsor the Christmas Dance this year. Much to my surprise, the students are up in arms. Who would have believed they would notice, much less care?

After class a group of students corners me at my desk with Betsy Hill and Leigh Ann Smith in the forefront. Bright, pretty and popular, both girls work with me on the school's yearbook.

"Mrs. Jernigan," Betsy says, "you've *always* sponsored the dance. I'll just die if you don't this year."

She's president of Thespians and the star of every school play. I can see why. She has real tears in her eyes, and she looks devastated. If she's *not* acting, then I'm far more important to her than I ever dreamed.

"*Please*," Leigh Ann says. "You're the only one we can *talk* to."

"I'm sure Miss Laney would do a wonderful job," I tell them. "She's young. You'll enjoy her."

"She never *listens*," Leigh Ann says, while Betsy rolls her eyes and grimaces. "You always *care* about what we say and you *never* make us feel silly or stupid or *wrong*."

Leigh Ann's habit of speaking in italics can enchant you or irritate you. I consider this intensity as one of her most endearing qualities.

"Please," they say at the same time.

"I haven't said no. I've said I'll have to think about it."

After school another group waylays me in the parking lot to beg that I reconsider. I'd talk to Patsy about this if we were still confidantes. Until Harry came along she had an innate ability to view situations with clear eyes and a level head.

Maybe I'll talk to her anyway. Since she's not emotionally invested in the Christmas dance, it would be the perfect excuse to keep the doors of communication open.

The idea perks me up, and as I round the corner to my street, the colors of fall spill through me and settle into my breastbone with a sigh. *Yes.* The extravagant beauty of the changing seasons continues, no matter what. We can quiet our souls and appreciate the splendor or we can immerse ourselves so deeply into our own petty quarrels that we might as well be living in a cave.

This residential area is one of the oldest in Tupelo, so most of the trees are ancient, stately blackjack oaks and lichen-covered pecans. But a

few of them are young maples that put on a vivid
display of red and yellow and gold in October.

I stand in my front yard awhile and simply
breathe, then I go inside, perk a cup of hazelnut
vanilla coffee, pour it in a gold-rimmed china cup
and add real cream. Kicking off my shoes, I stand
in a spot of sunshine beside my kitchen window
and savor the taste. It's these simple pleasures—
fall leaves and rich, gourmet coffee—that make us
believe God's in his heaven and all is right with
the world. And if things aren't exactly perfect in
our lives, if we're moving backward instead of
forward, then these small treats make us believe
we can correct, adjust, compromise and adapt
until we are headed in the right direction.

Taking my coffee, I go into the office and turn
on my computer.

From: "The Lady" louisejernigan@yahoo.com
To: "Miss Sass" patsyleslie@hotmail.com
Date: Monday, October 30, 4:00 p.m.
Subject: Christmas Dance
You're not going to believe what happened at
school today. I told the principal I want to recon-

sider sponsoring the Christmas dance, and the students set up such a protest you'd think they'd had their cars taken away. What's going on? Surely they wouldn't miss this old fuddy-duddy if I decided to bow out.
Louise


Patsy's still at work so I rub a rump roast with garlic and rosemary, put it in the oven and sit in my sunroom with my coffee and a stack of book reports.

At the insistence of Josh and her obstetrician, Diana stopped working two weeks ago and usually calls this time of day. But today I grade without interruption. She's driving home her point, letting me feel the coolness of her displeasure. It's working. Even the spectacular view of setting sun on golden leaves and Betsy Hill's report on *The Heart Is a Lonely Hunter* by Carson McCullers can't take my mind off the silent telephone and the tick of a clock marking the lonely march of time.

The report reminds me that we are all wounded, and we are all seeking a balm that will ease our pain. My pain is loneliness and the loss of dreams. Is it Patsy's, too, and is that why we both turned to a man who had a Band-Aid in his pocket but couldn't come close to providing the healing balm of constancy, caring and true tenderness?

The sound of Patsy's Jag makes me jump, and I want to race to the computer and stare at the screen until her reply pops up. Instead I sip my coffee—grown tepid but nonetheless satisfying—glance at a maple turned to flame by the setting sun and finish grading Betsy's book report.

Patsy will be taking off her shoes, refilling King Kong's water dish, putting a CD on her stereo—probably Elvis or Jerry Lee Lewis boogying to "Blue Suede Shoes" or "Great Balls of Fire."

Then she'll glance into her refrigerator, bite her lower lip because there's nothing inside except a head of wilting lettuce and leftovers, which I know she hates. She'll say "What the hell" then reach into her icebox for a frozen TV dinner. Fried chicken with English peas and mashed potatoes. A little smear of apple cobbler on the side.

I gather my papers, take the empty cup into the kitchen and rinse it under warm tap water, then finally go into my office and log onto e-mail. The satisfying ding that signifies mail waiting fills me with excitement. And hope.

From: "Miss Sass" patsyleslie@hotmail.com
To: "The Lady" louisejernigan@yahoo.com
Date: Monday, October 30, 6:00 p.m.
Subject: Re: Christmas Dance

I ought to take a broom to you. Don't you know by now that your students think you are the next best thing to pizza with everything on it? What's it going to take to make you realize that your life has counted for something? While I'm in that damn bank making change, you're at the high school changing lives.

And while we're on the subject of change, I've changed my mind about Harry Wayne Thompson. What a lying turd he turned out to be. And if you say "I told you so" I'm going to sneak into your house and dump all your gourmet coffee.

Guess who I visited today? Gloria. His Wednesday woman. Lord knows whether he has enough starch to satisfy Monday and Friday women, but if my last fling in his bed is any indication, I doubt it. In fact, I'd bet money on it.

Patsy, with egg on her face

From: "The Lady" louisejernigan@yahoo.com
To: "Miss Sass" patsyleslie@hotmail.com
Date: Monday, October 30, 6:05 p.m.
Subject: Re: Christmas Dance
Wipe that egg off. Everybody makes mistakes,
though I'll have to say you do it with more energy
and pizzazz than most folks.
How did you find out, and what did she do when
you confronted her?
Louise, dying of curiosity

From: "Miss Sass" patsyleslie@hotmail.com
To: "The Lady" louisejernigan@yahoo.com
Date: Monday, October 30, 6:10 p.m.
Subject: Re: Christmas Dance
She sent flowers to the sorry so-and-so. And he was
foolish enough to tell me she was his secretary at
City Hall. Well, you know me. I know so many people
down there I practically have an engraved invitation.
Today on my lunch hour I politely prissed myself
into her office and said, "Hello, I'm Harry Wayne
Thompson's Tuesday woman, and my friend
Louise is his Thursday woman." You could have
picked her up off the floor with a spoon. She
melted all over the place, squalling and sweating

and probably peeing in her pants, too. In spite of the fact that she was ten years younger and fifteen pounds lighter than me, I actually felt sorry for her. "If I were you," I said, "I'd march over there, grab my flowers then take them to Beautiful Bouquets and demand my wasted money back."

If I were the gloating kind, I'd celebrate with a glass of champagne, but even I have more character than that. What I ought to do is steal those tacky red carnations from Harry and take them to her as a consolation prize.

Patsy, self-righteously indignant but a bit sad, too

From: "The Lady" louisejernigan@yahoo.com
To: "Miss Sass" patsyleslie@hotmail.com
Date: Monday, October 30, 6:20 p.m.
Subject: Re: Christmas Dance

You have every right to be sad. You've lost the man you thought you loved. More than that, you've lost your dream of a future for two.

But you can find it again. And you still have me. This reminds me of New Orleans, of how mad we were but how we picked right up where we'd left off once we started speaking again. I never did know why you were so upset over a bartender you

didn't seem to care that much about. I was so glad to be friends with you again, I never did ask. I'm asking now.
Louise


From: "Miss Sass" patsyleslie@hotmail.com
To: "The Lady" louisejernigan@yahoo.com
Date: Monday, October 30, 6:27 p.m.
Subject: Re: Christmas Dance
I wasn't mad about the bartender. I left New Orleans because you were turning down men right and left and seemed bound and determined to devote the rest of your life to taking care of Josh and me. Even as selfish as I am I couldn't let that happen.
Thank God for Bill or we still might not be speaking. I realized I couldn't have a wedding without you.
Patsy


From: "The Lady" louisejernigan@yahoo.com
To: "Miss Sass" patsyleslie@hotmail.com
Date: Monday, October 30, 6:32 p.m.
Subject: Re: Christmas Dance
You mean we spent a whole year apart over that? Why didn't you tell me?
Louise

From: "Miss Sass" patsyleslie@hotmail.com
To: "The Lady" louisejernigan@yahoo.com
Date: Monday, October 30, 6:35 p.m.
Subject: Re: Christmas Dance
Would you have gone to that fabulous teaching
job in Alaska if I had?
Patsy

From: "The Lady" louisejernigan@yahoo.com
To: "Miss Sass" patsyleslie@hotmail.com
Date: Monday, October 30, 6:37 p.m.
Subject: Re: Christmas Dance
Probably not.
Louise

From: "Miss Sass" patsyleslie@hotmail.com
To: "The Lady" louisejernigan@yahoo.com
Date: Monday, October 30, 6:39 p.m.
Subject: Re: Christmas Dance
I rest my case. See, you're not always smarter than
I am.
Of course, at the moment I feel dumber than a
post oak. I haven't confronted Harry about Gloria
yet. Any suggestions?
Patsy

From: "The Lady" louisejernigan@yahoo.com
To: "Miss Sass" patsyleslie@hotmail.com
Date: Monday, October 30, 6:42 p.m.
Subject: Re: Christmas Dance
Yes. Revenge!
I've got a pot roast with new potatoes, green beans and Caesar salad. Come over and we'll lay our plans over dinner.
Louise

From: "Miss Sass" patsyleslie@hotmail.com
To: "The Lady" louisejernigan@yahoo.com
Date: Monday, October 30, 6:45 p.m.
Subject: Re: Christmas Dance
Now you're talking. Keep supper hot. I'll be right over.
Patsy, hungry for everything except Harry

## CHAPTER 16

*Patsy*

**What** I want to do is breeze through the hedge looking like somebody in charge of her life and say, I'm sorry I acted a fool. Then I'd make a clever joke of our misunderstanding, sit down at Louise's polished mahogany table and eat her good roast beef, which will feature rosemary.

She always uses fresh herbs, just as she always buys gourmet coffee. I've even missed these quirks of hers.

Naturally, what I do is fight my way through the overgrown hedges in my big black-cat house shoes and a fuzzy pink sweater that needed to go to Goodwill three years ago. But I couldn't give it away because wearing it feels like being cuddled by a good friend…Louise.

She's standing in the door with her gray roots beginning to show, and I don't have the slightest urge to tell her to get her color touched up. Plus, she's in these baggy pants that look like they're older than indoor plumbing. I decide, on the spot, to throw away my ridiculous Lycra miniskirts and get some pants just like hers, comfortable pants made for raking leaves in the fall, lounging around with your bare feet up to watch *The Golden Girls* and sitting in the middle of the bed eating popcorn with your best friend.

She probably found them in a yard sale. We'll check them out this Saturday. We'll wear Reeboks and old sweatshirts and no makeup. And if a spry-looking man with all his own teeth and hair and laugh lines around his eyes happens to glance our way, we won't even look.

"Patsy." That's all Louise says. Just Patsy.

And then she opens her arms and I fall into them and we stand in her open doorway swaying like seasoned oaks that weather rain and wind and drought and even know how to withstand an occasional tornado.

Finally she says, "Are you hungry?"

"Yes. Let's eat."

We go into her kitchen with arms linked because we know this is enough, this powerful bond of friendship that needs no words.

From: "The Lady" louisejernigan@yahoo.com
To: "Miss Sass" patsyleslie@hotmail.com
Date: Tuesday, October 31, 4:00 p.m.
Subject: Our Plan

Well, today I told Dr. Cramer I'd sponsor the Christmas dance, and word got out even before I got to my first-period class. Students came by my room and stopped me in the hall all day to tell me how much I've helped and inspired them and how happy they are that I'll be there at their annual holiday dance.

Lord, I had no idea I was so popular. I feel like Mr. Holland in that movie, *Mr. Holland's Opus.* You remember the story: the school music teacher thinks he's a failure because he never finished a symphony he'd been trying to write for twenty years. Then he realizes his opus is not his music, his students are.

I wish you were back from work so I could come over and tell you this in person. I feel as if I've taken a right turn somewhere without even knowing it, and all of a sudden I've risen up out of a drab rut and ended up on the scenic route.

About our plan...are you sure you want to go through with it? We don't have to, you know. We can just forget Harry Wayne Thompson exists and get on with our lives.

Louise

From: "Miss Sass" patsyleslie@hotmail.com
To: "The Lady" louisejernigan@yahoo.com
Date: Tuesday, October 31, 5:40 p.m.
Subject: Re: Our Plan

Don't you dare chicken out. I'm not about to let Harry Wayne Thompson get off scot-free after what he did to us. Dating both of us at the same time was bad enough, but nearly splitting us up was un-conscionable. Not only us, but our whole family.

I called Josh before I went to work this morning to put his mind at ease. With the baby due in a few weeks, they've got enough on their minds without worrying about us.

Patsy

P.S. I loved that movie, and if you'll care to remember, I've already told you that all these years you've been doing something wonderful. When you die I'm going to put a monument on your grave that reads, "She made a difference in lives."

From: "The Lady" louisejernigan@yahoo.com
To: "Miss Sass" patsyleslie@hotmail.com
Date: Tuesday, October 31, 5:45 p.m.
Subject: Re: Our Plan

Who says I'm going to die first? You always told me to make sure they bury you in that red suit you bought in Memphis. And I intend to. ?

No, I'm not backing out. I'll face the gossips at bridge while you (I assume) will see Harry Wayne.

Louise

P.S. I talked to Diana, too. She cried when I told her we were friends again. Poor little thing. I felt horrible for having put her through that.

From: "Miss Sass" patsyleslie@hotmail.com
To: "The Lady" louisejernigan@yahoo.com
Date: Tuesday, October 31, 5:50 p.m.

Subject: Re: Our Plan

Me, too. I ought to be covered with peanut butter and hung out for the birds. Ah, well, I'm not perfect but I'm entertaining.

"See" does not begin to describe what I'm going to do to Harry Wayne. When I've finished with him tonight, he's going to think I'm the Queen of Seduction and the Goddess of Foreplay. By the time I develop a "headache," he's going to be so hot and bothered he can't even walk me to the door. Whoops. Look at the time. I've got to get gorgeous and you've got to get to bridge. And for God's sake, don't run any stop signs.

Patsy

From: "The Lady" louisejernigan@yahoo.com
To: "Miss Sass" patsyleslie@hotmail.com
Date: Wednesday, November 1, 6:30 a.m.
Subject: Casanova

How did it go last night with Casanova?

Bridge was awful. By the time Mary Jo finished probing me for information I wanted to snatch a lock of her hair, come home and stick pins in a Voodoo doll.

Louise

From: "Miss Sass" patsyleslie@hotmail.com
To: "The Lady" louisejernigan@yahoo.com
Date: Wednesday, November 1, 6:35 a.m.
Subject: Re: Casanova
Exactly as planned. He never dreamed I wanted to cut off his most prized possession and back over it with my Jag.
Have you called him yet?
Patsy
P.S. I'm thinking of quitting bridge. I'm tired of shuffling cards and trying to keep points straight and NEVER winning. I don't know why I ever agreed to play it in the first place. I don't even like it.

From: "The Lady" louisejernigan@yahoo.com
To: "Miss Sass" patsyleslie@hotmail.com
Date: Wednesday, November 1, 6:40 a.m.
Subject: Re: Casanova
We used to play Rook all the time in New Orleans. Why didn't you tell me you don't like bridge?
Yes, I called him. He was excited about seeing me tomorrow night—that cad.
Louise

From: "Miss Sass" patsyleslie@hotmail.com
To: "The Lady" louisejernigan@yahoo.com

Date: Wednesday, November 1, 6:45 a.m.
Subject: Re: Casanova
Rook was fun. These barracudas at bridge play for
blood. I joined to please you. Besides, I didn't
have anything else to do.
Give Harry hell, girlfriend.
Patsy, trying to get to the rat race on time so
Herbert won't chew me out


From: "The Lady" louisejernigan@yahoo.com
To: "Miss Sass" patsyleslie@hotmail.com
Date: Wednesday, November 1, 4:00 p.m.
Subject: Honors
You'll never believe what happened at school
today. One of my students, Betsy Hill, made the
highest scored on the SAT test, and she named
me STAR teacher.
Betsy and I will be honored at the state banquet in
Jackson this Saturday. Do you want to go with me?
Louise


From: "Miss Sass" patsyleslie@hotmail.com
To: "The Lady" louisejernigan@yahoo.com
Date: Wednesday, November 1, 5:40 p.m.
Subject: Re: Honors

Are you kidding? My middle name is Go, especially when my best friend is being honored. What time do we need to leave?

Patsy

P.S. I'll do the driving.


From: "The Lady" louisejernigan@yahoo.com

To: "Miss Sass" patsyleslie@hotmail.com

Date: Wednesday, November 1, 5:50 p.m.

Subject: Re: Honors

Let's leave early. Say seven o'clock. That will give us enough time to shop and have lunch on the Ross Barnett Reservoir—fried hush puppies and catfish.

Louise


From: "Miss Sass" patsyleslie@hotmail.com

To: "The Lady" louisejernigan@yahoo.com

Date: Wednesday, November 1, 5:59 p.m.

Subject: Re: Honors

Seven, it is. By the way, I know a store in Jackson that's even bigger and better than Fantasy Land in Columbus. We can get everything we need for REVENGE!

If we don't do it for ourselves, let's do it for

Diana. Think of the stress she went through because of him. And what about Patsy Louise? Do we want our granddaughter to go through the same thing we did?
If we can teach one jerk a lesson, maybe the rest of them will catch on and stop it.
Patsy

*Patsy*

Thursday morning I wake up with the feeling that the last few weeks have been a bad dream and that Harry Wayne Thompson never even existed. But when I reach under my bed for my black-cat slippers and find one of his socks, I know I haven't been dreaming at all: I've just been making a fool of myself and messing up my life.

I take the scissors, pretend the sock is Harry's Prized Possession, and cut it to pieces. Then I eat a honey bun, get dressed and climb into my Jag.

*Thank God* everything's back to normal. Louise is on her front porch with her purse on her arm, King Kong's giving me the cold shoulder because I got him the wrong kind of Meow Mix, and Irma

June Lipincott is mincing down the street with a pair of binoculars so everybody will think she's bird-watching instead of spying.

But as I round the corner of Robins and head toward the bank, I realize everything is not back to normal. I'm not the same woman who pranced into the bank every day thinking of ways I could get Herbert's goat without getting fired. I'm not the same person who settled for a life of building up a pension while I cashed checks and counted out change.

For all Harry Wayne's flaws—and they are myriad—he made me catch a glimpse of possibilities, and I'm not willing to let that vision go. I sit in my car in the parking lot and think about my future. A radical departure for me. Advance planning.

Even if I don't work thirty years, I've built up a nice 401K at the bank, and Bill had the foresight to put a big chunk of money for me in an IRA so I can't touch it now without paying a hefty fine. Plus, in a few years there'll be Social Security, a mixed blessing—having extra money but having to admit your real age.

When I finally sashay into the bank, Herbert attempts to dash my good mood with her worst scowl.

"You're late, Patsy. I'll have to dock fifteen minutes off your lunch hour."

"I won't be here for lunch. I quit."

I whiz past her and go upstairs to take care of paperwork that will make me a free woman. I feel like a butterfly emerging from its cocoon.

I treat myself to a cappuccino at Starbucks, revel in not having to push my way through late-afternoon and evening crowds at Wal-Mart where I get King Kong's favorite Meow Mix, imagine myself in caftan and sandals with turquoise-encrusted straps sipping the green tea chai I buy at Serenity, then dash into The Main Attraction and spend a giddy hour trying on hats and peasant skirts that swirl around my ankles and make me feel like a tall, blond version of Barbra Streisand.

A block up the street, I see the marquee of Tupelo Community Theater is announcing auditions for *Hello Dolly*.

Why not? My pipes may not be what they were when I was belting out the blues at LuLu's, but I can still sing. And I most certainly know how to strut my stuff.

I wander down Broadway and stand in front of the theater, picturing myself as Dolly Levi on this stage. It's not New York City, but it's still greasepaint and an orchestra pit and the camaraderie of kindred spirits putting together a show.

Of course, they don't pay a penny. Except for the theater manager, this is an all-volunteer organization, which leaves me with the big question: how will I earn money?

Not that I'm desperate, but what if I outlive my money?

I will not let this sobering thought dampen my spirits. Instead I drive to Birmingham Ridge to talk with Aunt Charlotte. To most of the world, she appears to be an eccentric kook in a John Deere T-shirt; but to me she's surrogate mother, friend and trusted advisor rolled into one.

Most people her age look back with regret on the chances they didn't take, the places they didn't go, the passion they didn't share. Not Aunt Charlotte. She lives every day fully and richly. And she does it her way.

Louise has a book that fits Aunt Charlotte to a T: it's called *I Will Not Die an Unlived Life*. I don't know if it's prose or poetry: All I know is that every time I see the title I want to jump up and shout, *Yes, yes.*

I park the Jag and go into the kitchen because nobody hears me knocking. Uncle Bradley hugs me then says Aunt Charlotte's whizzing around the back forty on her new John Deere Gator.

"Have some cake and coffee while you wait," he says.

"I'm not all that hungry."

He laughs. "Don't worry. Louise made the cake and I made the coffee."

"In that case, I'll have some."

"I hope you don't mind waiting here by yourself. My sister's complaining of back pains and I've got to drive over there and see about her before she worries herself to death."

"Not at all." I hug him, then kick my shoes off and eat cake. Two pieces. I need all the fuel I can get to keep pace with Aunt Charlotte.

She bustles in smelling like fall sunshine and sweet-clover hay, her color high and her hair sticking from underneath her cap like tossed-about dandelions.

"Either the government's declared another holiday named for somebody I never heard of, or you're in deep doo-doo." She cuts herself a hunk of cake and winks at me. "Which is it, Patsy girl?"

"Deep doo-doo."

"Good for you. Pour me some more coffee and let's talk about it."

By the time she's ready for a second cup, I've told about my jobless, uncertain future.

"What took you so long, Patsy? You never did belong behind a teller's window."

"Trying to blend in?"

"Piffle, you'll never blend in. Remember what you said when you and Josh came here looking like two lost puppies?"

"I told you so many things I don't remember."

"You said, 'Aunt Charlotte, I don't give a rat's butt about the opinion of strangers. I live for my son and my music.' There's no question about your loyalty to Josh, but it's high time for you to get back to your music."

Her words settle into my soul like the long-forgotten fragrance of an English rose. I breathe in the perfume of promise and smile.

"Do you have any suggestions, Aunt Charlotte?"

"I thought you would never ask."

## CHAPTER 17

From: "The Lady" louisejernigan@yahoo.com
To: "Miss Sass" patsyleslie@hotmail.com
Date: Thursday, November 2, 9:45 p.m.
Subject: Act I
Harry fell for Act I—my performance as liberated, woman-of-the-world with a libido as sweet and hot as my pear pie, all done with smoke and mirrors. Thank goodness I didn't have to prove anything. That second helping of pie slowed him down, and I was wearing Reeboks or I never would have outrun him when he started chasing me around the kitchen table.

Finally he got so winded he gave up, but he's salivating for Act II.

Louise, not quite gloating because I actually feel sorry for the oversexed geezer

P.S. So how was your day?

From: "Miss Sass" patsyleslie@hotmail.com
To: "The Lady" louisejernigan@yahoo.com
Date: Thursday, November 2, 9:48 p.m.
Subject: Re: Act I
I thought you'd never get home! I've been dying to tell you... I told Herbert to go jump in the lake, made long-range plans with Aunt Charlotte to turn her barn into a studio for the arts and bought some Sheetrock and four gallons of sunshine-yellow paint. While you were setting the hook with Harry, Aunt Charlotte brought her new farm manager to my house and we knocked out the wall between my dining room and my spare bedroom. I'm turning it into a studio for Patsy's Piano and Vocals, Private Lessons.
How about them apples!
Patsy, flying at last

From: "The Lady" louisejernigan@yahoo.com
To: "Miss Sass" patsyleslie@hotmail.com
Date: Thursday, November 2, 10:03 p.m.
Subject: Re: Act I
I'm flabbergasted. But then I always knew you had courage. I'll come over after school tomorrow and help you paint.

I knew Aunt Charlotte had been looking for a new manager ever since Lefty Loredo retired, but I didn't know she had found one. What's he like?
Louise

From: "Miss Sass" patsyleslie@hotmail.com
To: "The Lady" louisejernigan@yahoo.com
Date: Thursday, November 2, 10:06 p.m.
Subject: Re: Act I
I have no idea. He's nice, and that's all I care about. It'll be a cold day in July before I even look twice at another man.
By the way, did you set up the date with Harry for Act II? Or do you want me to do it next Tuesday?
Patsy
P.S. Thanks for the offer. I'll put on some Frank Sinatra records while we paint and we can sing along.

From: "The Lady" louisejernigan
To: "Miss Sass" patsyleslie@hotmail.com
Date: Thursday, November 2, 10:10 p.m.
Subject: Re: Act I
Act II IS next Tuesday. At the motel on Gloster.
Louise

P.S. You sing along and I'll tap my foot. You know I can't carry a tune in a bucket.

From: "Miss Sass" patsyleslie@hotmail.com
To: "The Lady" louisejernigan@yahoo.com
Date: Thursday, November 2, 10:12 p.m.
Subject: Re: Act I
I can teach you. Do you want to be my first student?
Patsy

From: "The Lady" louisejernigan@yahoo.com
To: "Miss Sass" patsyleslie@hotmail.com
Date: Thursday, November 2, 10:15 p.m.
Subject: Re: Act I
Why not? I need to branch out. After we finish with Harry, we could schedule my lessons for Tuesday nights. It will give us something to do besides bridge.
Louise

From: "Miss Sass" patsyleslie@hotmail.com
To: "The Lady" louisejernigan@yahoo.com
Date: Thursday, November 2, 10:17 p.m.
Subject: Re: Act I
You're quitting bridge?!!
Patsy, planning to turn you into a songbird

From: "The Lady" louisejernigan@yahoo.com
To: "Miss Sass" patsyleslie@hotmail.com
Date: Thursday, November 2, 10:20 p.m.
Subject: Re: Act I
You said you were thinking about quitting, and quite frankly, I'm tired of it, too. The same old cards, the same old crowd, the same old gossip. Louise, who is tired of being predictable and has decided to spice up her life…but not with another Harry Wayne

*Louise*

My fishnet stockings itch, my corset pinches and my shelf bra lifts my breasts practically to my chin. Mincing across the room in knee-high red patent-leather boots with four inch heels, I call my partner in crime.

"Patsy, hurry up before I pass out. I don't know how I let you talk me into this getup."

I bought every bit of my ridiculous garb in Jackson. Me. A STAR teacher. I just hope I don't see one of my students tonight. Or worse, a parent.

"I'll be there as soon as I can suck in enough stomach to zip this catsuit."

Patsy decided to go as Cat Woman in a black leather bra and low-slung pants I couldn't squeeze my left thigh into. When she walks through my front door and flings open her trench coat, I almost feel envy. It's unnatural for a woman her age to look that good.

"What do you think?" she says.

"I think Harry Wayne is going to believe he's died and gone to that great brothel in Hades. Did you call him?"

"Yes. He's in room 131 waiting. Grab your coat, girlfriend. It's showtime."

"I hope 131 is at the back of the hotel."

I climb into the Jag, making sure my trench coat doesn't fly open to shock and entertain the neighbors.

"It doesn't matter, I brought these." Patsy puts on a wide-brimmed felt hat that hides most of her face, then tosses one to me.

We head toward Gloster Street and Operation Revenge.

*Patsy*

Just think. The man I thought I loved and wanted to be with the rest of my life is waiting for a ménage à trois. When he grabs Louise and me for a three-partner hug, I want to ram my knee into his prized privates.

Instead I blow in his ear and purr, "Are you ready for some fun?"

"I can hardly wait. If I'd known the two of you were so continental, we'd have been doing this a long time ago."

*In a pig's eye.* It's too soon to kick Harry, so I kick the door shut instead. Louise jerks it open and hangs the Privacy Please sign, then we fling open our raincoats.

"Let's party," I say.

"Bring it on, baby," Louise says.

I didn't know she had it in her. She's prancing and jiggling like a barmaid in a black-and-white Western. Not to be outdone, I uncoil the whip hanging from my belt and crack it in the air two inches from Harry's café au lait birthmark I used to think was cute. Now all I'm thinking is that he could use an hour a day on the treadmill.

He jumps like somebody who was scared into next Tuesday, then tries to cover it up by doing a spastic strip dance across the room. Louise rolls her eyes behind his back while I grind my heel on his fallen Jockey shorts.

"Let's get this over with," I whisper.

"Come on, big boy."

*Lord*, who taught Louise to purr and growl like that? As soon as I get her out of here, I'm going to find out.

"You two babes strip. I've got a little surprise for you."

Harry reaches into the dresser drawer, then whirls around and says, "Taa-daa."

"Green scarves." I try to act impressed.

"Not red," Louise says, making it sound like she's seen the eighth wonder of the world.

"Hop in bed, girls."

"No." Prancing toward the bed like somebody with the Fourth of July in her pushup bra, Louise pulls back the covers. "You hop in, Harry. We're the ones with the surprise."

There he goes. Slithering between the sheets like the snake he is. I whip out my handcuffs and chain his wrists to the bedposts, while Louise lashes down his legs with his own green silk scarves.

Tossing Louise the whip, I say, "You take the first whack."

Harry's lecherous grin falters. "Just fun and games? Right, babe?"

Ignoring him, Louise tosses the whip back to me.

"No, Patsy. You go first."

I give the whip another sharp crack. My stint as Annie Oakley in the high school drama is finally paying off. Sweat beads line Harry's upper lip, and his smile has completely vanished.

"Okay, girls. Be easy now. I'm not the young buck I used to be."

"What do you think, Louise, should we take it easy on this two-timing alleycat?" I pop the whip close enough to singe his receding hairline.

"I don't think so. Let's give him a few licks for Gloria, too."

Harry's sweating in earnest now, but at least he has enough sense to keep his mouth shut. I run the butt of the whip down his chest and rest it on his groin, giving it just enough pressure to make him grunt.

"On second thought, I don't think he's worth our time." I roll the whip and hang it back on my belt.

"You've got that right, Patsy."

As we head toward the door he yells, "Wait a minute. Where are you going?"

"To dinner," Louise says.

"What about these?" He strains against his handcuffs. I almost feel sorry for the old coot.

"Don't worry. The hotel's cleaning staff will unlock you in the morning."

I put the key to the cuffs on the dresser and nab the key he won't be using. Then we don our trench coats and walk out. Neither of us says a word till we're in my Jag.

"Where to, Louise? Kentucky Fried or Burger King?"

"Burger King. I need red meat."

"Me, too. All that stress."

At the drive-through we order the biggest burgers they have, and decide to eat right there in the parking lot.

"I don't know about you," Louise says, "but I feel exhilarated, liberated. We ought to call ourselves the Granny Avengers and go into business. Think of the wronged women who would flock to us."

"Leave the granny part out, and I'm all for it."

We concentrate on our food for a while, and then Louise says, "Seriously, though, now that it's all over, I'm actually feeling sorry for him."

"I'm too selfish for that kind of compassion."

"You are *not*. What are you feeling, Patsy? You had higher expectations with him than I did."

"Sad, mostly. I can't help but think how nice it would have been if he had turned out even half as wonderful as Rocky."

"Don't let one rotten apple spoil the whole barrel for you."

"You? Resorting to clichés? I can't believe it."

"I used my creative quota putting on that show at the motel." She sips her chocolate milk shake, then takes the top off and digs for the ice cream with her straw. "Patsy, what if he has to go to the bathroom?"

"Or chokes to death in his own acid reflux?"

When I start the engine and head north on Gloster, Louise asks, "Are you going where I think you are?

"Yep. We've got to turn the big horse's butt loose. I think he's learned his lesson by now."

I wish I had a camera to record Harry's face when we sashay back into his room. It's the perfect picture of contrition and hope, a poster layout of a man brought to his knees by the women he played for fools.

"For the love of God," Harry yells. "If you two will leave me alone, I'll leave you alone."

"Now, Harry." I grab the key off the dresser. "Is that any way to talk to your liberators?"

I unsnap his handcuffs while Louise unties his legs. And then I nearly wet my pants when she intones, "Go and sin no more, Harry Wayne."

Now she's standing at the foot of his bed with that pursed-lipped, serious look she gets when she's fixing to deliver a moralistic lecture. I grab her arm and drag her to the door.

"Wait. I had a few things to tell Mr. Harry Wayne Thompson."

"Get in the car, Louise, before you get arrested for indecent exposure."

"Oh, My Lord." She grabs the end of her raincoat that's flapping in the sudden breeze, then bails into the car just as the first, fat raindrops hit the windshield.

I felt the chill of approaching winter in that breeze, and I can't wait to get home, take off my catsuit, pour myself a big glass of chardonnay and curl up on my sofa with King Kong—if he's in a sociable mood. If not, I'll curl up while he glares and switches his tail. It's his way of saying I have lots of shortcomings.

And I guess I do. But the good thing is, I'm learning to live with them. Heck, I'm even learning to label some of them eccentricities and love them. Who else could make Louise laugh the way I do simply by wearing house shoes that look like black cats? And how else could I help fill the void his father left if I didn't sweep through Josh's house with a larger-than-life attitude, an outrageous vocabulary and inappropriate clothes?

Tonight was cathartic for me. Oh, I know

Louise and I went over the top, but maybe it takes that kind of absurdity to purge you, to make you see that you're only human, you're entitled to mistakes, you're granted the right to look silly and selfish and desperate and afraid.

The trick is to move on, to remember the things worth keeping, and to do everything in your power to keep them—friendship and family and a tender self-regard that makes allowances for mistakes.

## CHAPTER 18

From: "The Lady" louisejernigan@yahoo.com
To: "Miss Sass" patsyleslie@hotmail.com
Date: Wednesday, November 8, 7:00 a.m.
Subject: Our Former Lover
Are you still okay about last night? I don't want you to feel bad.
Louise

From: "Miss Sass" patsyleslie@hotmail.com
To: "The Lady" louisjernigan@yahoo.com
Date: Wednesday, November 8, 7:10 a.m.
Subject: Re: Our Former Lover
I have no regrets. What I feel more than anything is emptied out. I'm feeling better than I have in a long time...about everything...myself, my future, even Harry.
Don't get alarmed. I'm not excusing what he did; I just don't wish him any harm. That's all.

Can you come over after school and paint? I think
we can finish my music room. I'll pick up chicken
salad at Finney's.
Patsy

From: "The Lady" louisejernigan@yahoo.com
To: "Miss Sass" patsyleslie@hotmail.com
Date: Wednesday, November 8, 7:12 a.m.
Subject: Re: Our Former Lover
Neither do I. For all we know, his heart could be
hurting with every beat.
You can count on me this afternoon to paint.
Louise

From: "Miss Sass" patsyleslie@hotmail.com
To: "The Lady" louisejernigan@yahoo.com
Date: Wednesday, November 8, 7:15 a.m.
Subject: Re: Our Former Lover
I can count on you. Period. ?
Patsy

*Louise*

I'm in gray sweats and bare feet, standing on a
ladder with a drop cloth underneath, putting the

finishing touch on the crown molding while Patsy finishes the baseboards and belts out the blues along with a CD by Li'l Rosie.

"'Ain't no use cryin', baby. The world done stomped us flat.'"

"Sing something cheerful, Patsy. There's a full moon coming and Patsy Louise is fixing to be born."

"Won't she love us? One grandma who's a STAR teacher and the other who's a star?"

Patsy got the role of Dolly Levi in Tupelo Community Theater's production of *Hello Dolly*. The theater manager posted the cast list today. She was so excited she called me during lunch period at school, and called Josh at work.

As if that weren't cause enough for celebration, her ad for Patsy's Private Piano and Vocals came out today, and she already has six students.

Josh and Diana sent yellow roses, and I brought over a bottle of chardonnay that's chilling in her ice bucket.

"I wish I could have seen your audition. When do rehearsals start?"

"Next week. Why don't you come along and

work on the stage crew? It would be a heck of a lot more fun than quilting."

Standing on the third rung with paint streaking Roy's blue-striped shirt and the tips of my spiky hairdo, I don't feel like the same woman I was four months ago. I'm not that white mouse who knew nothing except the familiar walls of her maze and the treat waiting at the finish line.

I'm learning to knock down the walls and grab my treats along the way, and so I tell Patsy yes.

She does a little victory dance while I yell, "Watch out. You're going to kick the bucket."

"Not a chance."

The paint bucket tumbles and I race off the ladder to help her clean up the mess.

"Thank God for a drop cloth," I say.

"Thank God for wings."

"Amen," I say, needing no explanation.

As we traipse toward the utility room to wash up, King Kong switches his tail and I switch mine right back.

"Bravo, Louise. You're really feeling your oats, girlfriend."

I guess I am. I've survived a trial by fire this fall and come through like well-tempered steel.

"I was just thinking," she says. "Why don't we join the Saturday Adventure Club and learn to have fun outdoors instead of being cooped up inside with a deck of cards or a needle and thread."

"Great. But you have to promise me one thing."

"What?"

"If you meet a man and decide to start dating again, the first thing you'll do is introduce him to your best friend."

"Done. You want to sign a blood pact?"

"Good Lord, Patsy. What I want to do is finish washing up, then open that chardonnay and celebrate."

"What are we celebrating?"

"Your starring role, your new profession, our pending grandmotherhood. Life. Us."

While we're still cleaning paintbrushes, the phone rings.

"Wouldn't you know? I'll bet it's Betty Lynn calling to pry about my ad."

While Patsy's in the kitchen on the phone, I

rinse the last of the paint off the brushes then grab the soap and start on my hands and arms. Over the rush of water I hear a muted murmur.

"Louise, come quick. Diana's in the hospital."

I drop the soap and hurry into the hall where Patsy, panicked, is already grabbing her purse and coat. It's a good thing I'm here.

"There's no need to rush. First labors take forever."

"No, we've got to go. Now."

"Patsy, calm down. It'll just take a few minutes to finish washing up and change clothes."

"There are complications, Louise."

"Oh my God."

Now I'm thanking my lucky stars that I'm at Patsy's, because if she hadn't reminded me to put on my shoes, I'd have barreled out the door barefoot in forty-degree weather. Lord, Lord, a Southerner can practically freeze to death in weather like that, especially a woman who puts on socks at the first sign of September.

When we're in the car racing down Gloster looking like two losers in a paint war, I recover enough to ask for particulars.

"I don't know. He just said *hurry*."

I look at the speedometer, which is creeping toward sixty in the forty-mile zone.

"If you hurry anymore we're going to end up with a ticket."

"I hope a cop does see me. I'll ask for an escort."

We don't get an escort. Thank God. What we do get is a stricken-looking Josh, who meets us in the lobby of the Women's Hospital with his hair standing on end from repeated nervous combing with his long fingers. He's so upset he doesn't even notice that the main thing we're wearing is yellow paint.

"Mama. Mama Two." He folds us in a desperate embrace while Patsy croons, "It's all right, son. Everything's going to be all right."

*Please*, God. The prayer circles around my mind like birds, and all I can think about is Diana at her first dance recital, beribboned and pink-cheeked, bursting into tears when she walked onstage. I finally caught her eye, and the minute she saw Roy and me on the front row, she settled into the dance routine and gave the best performance of the evening. Or so we thought.

*Please God, let her give the best performance of the evening.*

Josh leads us to hard plastic chairs in the waiting room where we drink tepid coffee from foam cups. I barely notice it's the cheap kind.

"The baby turned. It's breach," he says. "He didn't want to put more stress on the baby. Diana's having a C-section now."

We huddle together, silent, sipping coffee, reaching out to give reassuring pats, trying not to notice the minute hand inching around the huge clock on the wall, trying not to think of everything that could go wrong.

"Mr. Delgado?" The doctor is standing in the doorway in green scrubs, his mask hanging down his neck, his face serious.

Patsy looks the way I feel—ready to rush over, grab him by the collar and choke the news out of him. But this is Josh's wife, Josh's baby, Josh's moment. I catch her arm, hold her back while her son moves forward for the news.

"You have a healthy eight-pound, six-ounce baby boy."

Patsy whoops, I collapse on my chair and Josh says, "How's Diana?"

"The mother is doing fine. She's in recovery, but the nurse is bringing your son out to see you."

Josh grabs both of us again in a bear hug, and Patsy, ever the trooper says, "I don't suppose you'd consider calling him Patsy Louise."

"Not on your life." The nurse places a blue bundle in Josh's arms, and he peels the blanket back to show off our grandchild. "Meet your grandson—Rocky Jernigan Delgado."

It's a perfect name for the perfect baby. I let Patsy hold him first because she finally has another Rocky, someone who will love her unconditionally.

And when it's my turn, when Patsy and Josh leave arm in arm to get fresh coffee, I press my face against his soft pink cheek and whisper, "Look at him, Roy. A Jernigan through and through."

Aunt Charlotte and Uncle Bradley burst through the door, and she doesn't even comment on my paint-spattered appearance. What she does comment on is my obvious surprise.

"Josh called. You didn't think he'd leave the great grandparents out, now, did you?"

This is one of the things I love best about Aunt Charlotte: that she fills every vacancy in the family, both mine and Patsy's. She offers her finger, then chortles when the baby latches on.

"Would you look at that? I'll have this little slugger driving the John Deere in no time."

Uncle Bradley winks at me, and I wink back while visions of the future unfold: a little boy racing up the rich green hills of the farm, then spreading his arms like wings and rolling all the way back down, tumbling through the sweet grass, secure in the knowledge that he has family waiting at the bottom to pick him up if he falls, to dust his knees and kiss his hurts and applaud when he climbs the hill to do it all over again.

# Maggie Skerritt can't get away from weddings...

The P.I. is dodging her mother's plans to turn her upcoming wedding into an 800-guest circus and is investigating the murder of a runaway bride. With her own wedding jitters, and a sudden crisis of confidence about her profession, Maggie thinks staying single—and becoming a bartender—might be better choices after all....

# Wedding Bell Blues

## by Charlotte Douglas

**Available December 2006**
**TheNextNovel.com**

HN69

# Solitary confinement never looked so good!

Instant motherhood felt a lot like being under house arrest, until somewhere between dealing with a burned bake-sale project, PTA meetings and preteen dating, Kate realized she'd never felt so free.

# Motherhood Without Parole

## by Tanya Michaels

Available November 2006
TheNextNovel.com

HN65

# You can't give to others…
# until you give to yourself!

Supermom Abby Blake is going on strike. Having
made her stand, Abby's not about to let anyone
stop her—until her sworn enemy Cole whisks her
away to Paris for some R & R. When the sparks
start flying Abby thinks that maybe this "strike"
should grow into a year-round holiday….

# The Christmas Strike
## by Nikki Rivers

HARLEQUIN®
Next™

# If only Harvey the Wonder Dog could dig up the dirt on her ex!

The last person she expected to see at her husband's funeral was his other wife! Penny can't bring herself to hate his "wife" or toss his amazing piano-playing dog out on his rump. But thanks to her ex's legacy and Harvey's "amazing" trainer, Penny's ready to run with whatever curveball life throws at her!

# The Other Wife

## by Shirley Jump

HN68
Available November 2006
TheNextNovel.com

HARLEQUIN®
NeXt™

# You can't give to others…
# until you give to yourself!

Supermom Abby Blake is going on strike. Having
made her stand, Abby's not about to let anyone
stop her—until her sworn enemy Cole whisks her
away to Paris for some R & R. When the sparks
start flying Abby thinks that maybe this "strike"
should grow into a year-round holiday….

# The Christmas Strike

## by Nikki Rivers

Available December 2006
TheNextNovel.com

HN71

HARLEQUIN®

NExt™

# If only Harvey the Wonder Dog could dig up the dirt on her ex!

The last person she expected to see at her husband's funeral was his other wife! Penny can't bring herself to hate his "wife" or toss his amazing piano-playing dog out on his rump. But thanks to her ex's legacy and Harvey's "amazing" trainer, Penny's ready to run with whatever curveball life throws at her!

# The Other Wife
## by Shirley Jump

# REQUEST YOUR FREE BOOKS!

## 2 FREE NOVELS PLUS 2 FREE GIFTS!

**There's the life you planned. And there's what comes next.**

**YES!** Please send me 2 FREE Harlequin® NEXT™ novels and my 2 FREE mystery gifts. After receiving them, if I don't wish to receive any more books, I can return the shipping statement marked "cancel." If I don't cancel, I will receive 3 brand-new novels every month and be billed just $3.99 per book in the U.S., or $4.74 per book in Canada, plus 25¢ shipping and handling per book plus applicable taxes, if any*. That's a savings of over 20% off the cover price! I understand that accepting the 2 free books and gifts places me under no obligation to buy anything. I can always return a shipment and cancel at any time. Even if I never buy anything from Harlequin, the two free books and gifts are mine to keep forever.

156 HDN EF3R   356 HDN EF3S

Name _____ (PLEASE PRINT)

Address _____ Apt. #

City _____ State/Prov. _____ Zip/Postal Code

Signature (if under 18, a parent or guardian must sign)

### Order online at www.TryNEXTNovels.com

### Or mail to the Harlequin Reader Service®:

| IN U.S.A. | IN CANADA |
|---|---|
| P.O. Box 1867 | P.O. Box 609 |
| Buffalo, NY | Fort Erie, Ontario |
| 14240-1867 | L2A 5X3 |

Not valid to current Harlequin NEXT subscribers.

**Want to try two free books from another line?**
**Call 1-800-873-8635 or visit www.morefreebooks.com**

* Terms and prices subject to change without notice. NY residents add applicable sales tax. Canadian residents will be charged applicable provincial taxes and GST. This offer is limited to one order per household. All orders subject to approval. Credit or debit balances in a customer's account(s) may be offset by any other outstanding balance owed by or to the customer. Please allow 4 to 6 weeks for delivery.

NEXT06

# Nora's life was changing at a pace faster than the Indy 500...

Her birthday a whisper away, she had her first hot flash and was prematurely becoming a grandmother. But going from primo designer to a prime suspect in one day is a bit too much—leading her to discover that older doesn't mean wiser. It just means feeling more free to be yourself.

# Change of Life

## by Leigh Riker

HARLEQUIN®

Ne<sup>™</sup>xt

Available December 2006
TheNextNovel.com

HN72